MURDER'S MASQUERADE
THE COMPLETE CASES OF
MIKE & TRIXIE, VOLUME 1

THE **ARGOSY** ™ LIBRARY

MURDER'S MASQUERADE
THE COMPLETE CASES OF MIKE
& TRIXIE, VOLUME 1

T.T. FLYNN

COVER BY
C.C BEALL

ILLUSTRATED BY
JOSEPH A. FARREN

POPULAR PUBLICATIONS · 2021

TABLE OF CONTENTS

THE DEADLY ORCHID

Detective Harris Sighed Dreamily as
Gloria Whitney Pressed Her Delicate Body
Close to Him—But He Had Been Warned
She Was as Dangerous as a Cobra

THOMPSON, EASTERN MANAGER of the Blaine Agency, said to me in the hotel room in Jacksonville, "Do dames fall for towheads like you, Mike?"

"Dames fall for anyone with a good line," I said, and waited. Six years' sleuthing with the Blaine agency had taught me that a fellow never knew what was coming next.

"You'll need a good line," Thompson grinned, fishing an old cigar stub out of his vest pocket. "There's a dame in Palm Beach who's responsible for the deaths of two men that we know of. And she's about ready to put a third scalp in her belt. I want you to meet her."

"Says you," I told him. "Figuring me for the third corpse, I suppose?"

"You never can tell." Thompson scraped a match under the edge of his chair and sucked on the cigar, rolling an eye at me as sober as a deacon.

"Who is this female execution squad—and where do I come in?" I asked him.

"She was baptized Gloria Whitney and has a string of aliases. Her nickname is the Orchid. Her specialty is blackmail. When she hooks a man he may as well pay up, take it on the front page, or write his own ticket. They fished one of her boy friends out of the river below New Orleans, and found another in his Park Avenue apartment with a bullet through his head. Not a bit of proof to connect the Orchid with either, of course. But there's no law against guessing."

"They should call her Aconite, the poison flower," I wise-cracked. "And what do I do with this hothouse assassin?"

Thompson rolled the cigar to the corner of his mouth and grinned at me. "I'm counting on that well known sex appeal of yours I've been hearing about from Trixie Meehan."

I damned Trixie Meehan for spreading those yarns. She panned me every chance she got.

Thompson grinned again, and then became serious.

"The Orchid is one of the smoothest crooks in the country, Mike. She makes big money and makes it easy. As near as we can find out, she's got a partner or so who don't show often. She's been in Palm Beach for a month, and made a killing—all but the collecting."

"Or the suicide," I suggested.

"Exactly!" Thompson snapped. "I talked to the poor devil this morning. It won't take much to make him reach for a gun. He's Waldo Maxwell of the State Trust."

"Not the Waldo Maxwell?"

"None other," Thompson assured me. "No fool like an old widower, and he took it hook, line and sinker, and put it on paper. He won't stand a chance in court. And it will cost him a cool quarter of a million to buy back the evidence."

"Holy catfish!" I gasped. "What a haul! Why doesn't he take the publicity and save the dough?"

"Be yourself!" Thompson said. "He'd be the laughing stock of the country. Men who formerly trusted his judgment would think him doddering and senile. No telling what it would do to his financial strength. Not to speak of

*"They're gone! Every stone and setting; while
you played the fool and I played bridge"*

winding up a distinguished career as the country's prize
clown. He'll pay if we can't settle it some other way."

Thompson was right. Waldo Maxwell had been a
national figure for forty years. His bank was a Gibraltar of
finance; he was the ultimate in conservative respectabil-
ity. He'd be finished, out, if the scandal sheets got a thing
like this.

"Maxwell retained the Blaine Agency," Thompson
continued. "The sky is the limit on expense. And we're
giving it to you. The Orchid is at the Palm Beach Palo
Verde, registered as Miss Gloria Dean and maid. We don't
know anything about the maid. It's a cinch she's crooked
too. Got any ideas?"

"Plenty," I said, thinking fast. "First, make good on that
expense account. And I'll want a good looking woman with
brains. Got one this side of New York?"

"Trixie Meehan is due here in the morning from Chicago. She'll work with you."

I groaned, knowing Trixie.

Next morning I bought luggage, evening clothes, dress shirts, shoes, hats, all the clutter an oil millionaire from west Texas would be likely to have.

Trixie Meehan blew in, had a conference with Thompson before he left town, did some whirlwind shopping herself. We made the train together with enough luggage to do a theatrical troupe.

AN HOUR BEFORE dinner that evening we rolled into Palm Beach in two taxis, one packed with luggage. The Palo Verde was four stories high, with sprawling wings, acres of velvet lawns and a golf course; shrubbery, flower beds, palms, and the blue surf of the open Atlantic creaming in on the white sand beach before it. We wheeled up a wide shell driveway and stopped before a long marquee. Four uniformed bellboys ran out to meet us.

Trixie kicked me on the ankle.

"Out, ape!" she hissed under her breath. "Husbands always help the little woman tenderly."

"There you go!" I snarled. "Trying to start something right off the bat!"

"Yes, darling," cooed Trixie for the driver's benefit as I helped her out to the sidewalk.

Trixie Meehan was a little frail slip of a thing with forget-me-not eyes, a knock 'em dead face, and a clinging vine manner that covered concentrated hell. She had a razor tongue, muscles like steel springs, a brain that made me dizzy at times, and absolutely no fear. And here she was cuddling close and cooing up into my face while the taxi driver eyed me like a sap.

I paid him and left the baggage for the bellhops.

"Lay off that googoo talk when you don't have to use it," I growled as we went into the lobby. "You get my goat."

Trixie grabbed my arm and snuggled close. "You big strong he-man!" she sighed.

I couldn't shove her there in the lobby, so I took it out on the clerk. "A suite. Two bedrooms. Best you have. Ocean exposure, on the third floor, if possible."

"A *quiet* suite, dear," Trixie trilled.

"A *quiet* suite!" I snapped to the clerk.

"I think we have one that will be entirely satisfactory," he beamed at me. "And I can give it to you for only eighty dollars a day, since this is late in the season."

"Eighty a what?" I gagged.

"Eighty dollars a day," the clerk repeated firmly, and managed to chill me with one eye while he eyed our mountainous luggage, just coming in, with the other.

Trixie pinched my arm, and smiled brightly. "Eighty dollars a day is quite satisfactory, darling," she cooed. "Can't you remember that we have oil wells now?"

The clerk caught it. His face cleared instantly. He handed me a registry card and a fountain pen. I registered Mr. and Mrs. Blaine, San Antonio, Texas.

We looked like wealthy young globe trotters, for our old luggage was plastered with labels from everywhere. Undercover work for the Blaine Agency means travel. When the bellhops got their toll and left us alone in the suite, I went to the connecting door of the bedrooms and moved the key to my side.

"Verboten," I grunted at Trixie. "None of your blasted tricks now. I want some peace on this case."

Trixie threw her hat on the bed and made a face at me. "Be yourself, ape. Nobody's pursuing you. What has your massive brain planned for this evening?"

"The Orchid and her maid have three rooms at the end of the hall," I snapped. "I meet her, I make her, and then we take her."

"Just as easy as that," Trixie marveled. "Well, here's hoping. But don't forget we're married, darling, and I get some of this Palm Beach whoopee."

"Nix," I grinned. "That's for me and the Orchid. You're the neglected wife who mopes in her room."

"You'll have whiskers to your ankles when I do that," Trixie said through her teeth.

THE IDLE RICH! The wisecracker who said that never had more than a week's pay on hand in his life. Golf, tennis, swimming, riding, dancing—and bridge thrown in whenever Trixie could scare up a game. Three days of that to put us in the public eye and get our lines out.

The unlimited expense account made it possible; oil millionaires from Texas, hicks from the sticks, lathery with money. Trixie shopped at those exclusive little Fifth Avenue branch shops. They came to the hotel collect, and we had war the first night.

"Whose little gold digger are you?" I yelped. "Look at these bills I settled today! I knew you were a tough case, but I didn't know you had mucilage fingers. Any dumbwit you drag to the altar will be going for a cleaning instead of a honeymoon. Sixty-seven berries for a hat, and I could wear it for a felt thumb protector!"

"So!" said Trixie with a glitter in her eye. "You were snooping in my packages like a second story mug, Michael Harris?"

"When I pay sixty-seven crackers for a cardboard box and four yards of tissue paper and ribbon, I want to see what I'm stung with!" I gave her.

And Trixie moved in close for battle.

"Listen to me, you sack of wind! Nobody ever dragged you to the altar and they never will. Pull those popeyes in and get this straight! I'll send the beach up here collect if I feel like it, and you'll pay and thank me. Whose bank account is getting nicked? Not yours! Hand you a five dollar bill and you'd start jawing J.P. Morgan. Gold digger, am I, for providing a little atmosphere? Next time I hear a—"

I slammed the door on the rest. That acid tongue of Trixie's could lift the skin off a cigar store Indian.

We buried the subject of clothes. After all it wasn't my money. I took a flier or so in the market those three days. And the tips I ladled out everywhere disturbed my sleep nights. But they were good advertising. By the second day every flunkey in sight was bowing and scraping when I appeared. Funny how oil millions can spread. We were the gossip of the hotel. Some turned up their noses, and some fell over themselves to gladhand us.

The Orchid did neither.

I spotted her the first evening in the dining room, and the waiter cinched it. "That is Miss Dean, sir."

"Pretty girl to be dining alone."

"Miss Dean seldom has anyone at her table, sir. She is, if

I may be so free, a retiring woman." And the waiter rolled an expectant eye at Trixie.

"Perhaps, dear," says Trixie sweetly, "you would like to leave me and join her?"

And the waiter went off satisfied.

The Orchid had everything Thompson had outlined. I didn't try to guess her age. She was like an orchid, slender, graceful, dainty, fragile. She was a natural blonde—Trixie admitted that reluctantly—with a shell pink complexion and ripe red lips. Her eyelashes were long and dreamy, her makeup a bit of art, her expression tender and demure.

One look at her there in dainty solitude and I was willing to swear Thompson was a liar and Waldo Maxwell a lecherous old reprobate. A second look and I was hardboiled again. I've seen enough crooks to have an extra sense about them. Her eyes wandered over and caught my grin. She took me in from hair to second button on my dinner coat, and then went on eating, without a change of expression. But my neck hairs stiffened. She was like a beautiful leopard, lazily lapping cream. Claws were sheathed behind that fragile daintiness.

Trixie was on tap as usual. "All right, cave man, go into your act," she said under her breath.

"Rats to you," I said. "This is going to take technique."

The waiter returned and Trixie cooed: "Yes, dear." And we had honeymoon the rest of the dinner.

I didn't make a move for three days. But now and then when the Orchid was on the horizon I caught her studying me. The wild and woolly west, with a wagon load of money, and extra luggage in the wife, had come to Palm Beach. I spent as little time with Trixie as possible. I ogled the women when the Orchid was around. I flashed the bankroll and made a fool of myself. Anyone with half an eye could see I was ripe picking for a smart dame.

But it was Palmer, a natty customers' man for Trenholme and Edwards' branch brokerage office, who gave me my break. A little about oil wells and flyers in the market made him my man. He was a good looking young chap, a little too soft and polite; but he knew his Palm Beach, and the Orchid by sight when I pointed her out on the hotel veranda.

"Corker, isn't she?" Palmer sighed. "Haven't met her, but I hope to. See her all the time at Corey's. Say, that's a place you might like. Been there yet?"

"A big gambling joint, isn't it?"

"Yes.

"I'll be glad to take you and Mrs. Blaine there any time."

"Tonight," I said. "Mrs. Blaine will be busy. We'll go alone."

I'D HEARD ABOUT Corey's place; to gambling what Palm Beach was to society. With its clientele a Broadway gambler would have retired in six months. Strict cards of admission were required, and your name almost had to be in the social register to get one. Formal evening dress, of course, and once inside the old lavishly furnished frame building, set back in a tangle of trees and tropical growth, the sky was the limit. Private rooms upstairs for really high play. The drinks and food were on the house. The service was in keeping with the crowd who went there.

Palmer got a card some way. Things like that were his business. I went with a fat billfold, a boiled shirt, tails and everything—and tried to forget that in a few weeks I might be impersonating a longshoreman around the East River docks.

It was a joy to lose the first three hundred of someone else's money. We shifted from game to game for an hour and a half. Cool, perfumed air, beautiful women—some of them—men whose names made the newspapers, the hum and chatter of conversation, the quiet voices of the house men, now and then a black dressed automaton moving about with a tray. But no Orchid.

And then she came in, wrapped in a black coat with a roll of white around the collar. Stunning? I skipped a breath. "Palmer," I said, "I'm going to need the rest of the evening to myself. Would you mind ordering a Rolls outside in case I need it?"

And I went to the roulette table where the Orchid had drifted. For a few minutes I watched her lose five dollar chips, and then I slipped into an empty place at her side and slapped down five hundred. I lost and raised it to a thousand. And won, and won the next time, and the next. By that time I had the Orchid and everyone else at the table with me.

A fifty dollar bill was slipped into my palm, and I met a cool smile. "Will you play it?" the Orchid asked. "I think you are lucky tonight."

We won together.

Since it wasn't my money I didn't get the cold chills as I pushed my luck. I played the Blaine oil wells in public that night, and had the customers hanging on the edge of the table and standing three deep behind us. No, I didn't break the bank. They tell me no one ever does that at Corey's. But

I put on a good show, won six thousand when the plays were evened up, and broke the ice with the Orchid.

I stuffed the winnings in my pocket and grinned at the Orchid. "I always quit while I'm cool, ma'am. Would a little drive along the ocean front cap your luck?"

"It might," the Orchid agreed as she folded her cut. "Shall we try it?"

The motor of that big Rolls purred, and so did the Orchid. Her technique would have made Delilah quit. "You were so calm over those big stakes," she sighed.

"Shucks, ma'am, back in Texas, our stud games would make that piker play tonight."

"You're from Texas?"

"West Texas," I gave her breezily.

"Out in the oil country."

"How fascinating! Have you an oil well?"

"A dozen," I grinned. "An' two more spudding-in this week on proved ground. I always told Susan that when I passed my first million I was coming to Palm Beach. And here I am. But I never thought I'd be riding around with a beautiful woman like you."

"You flatter me," said the Orchid absently. "Your wife— does she like it? I've noticed her. She's a beautiful little thing."

"Susan's pretty enough," I agreed without enthusiasm. "But she says she'd rather be back home where she can be a big frog in a little puddle instead of a little frog in a big puddle like she is here."

The Orchid laughed softly.

"Perhaps she is right at that. A woman has to be used to this life before she can get the most out of it. I owe you more thanks than I can repay for making it possible for me to stay here a little longer."

"I don't understand," I mumbled, and waited for her line.

"The money you won for me," she explained. "That was almost my last fifty dollars I gave you."

"I thought you were—"

"—rich?" She laughed shortly. What an actress! "One thinks that about everyone here. A little insurance money can create quite an effect. But when it's gone—" She broke off on a quaver.

I put a hand over hers. "I understand."

"I thought you would," the Orchid murmured. "Now forget about me and tell me about Texas."

So I spun her a few yarns about how I started as a poor kid in the oil fields and finally got in the money. When I spoke about oil field life she looked out the window, and when I mentioned big money she was all ears again.

"I want you to meet Susan," I said finally.

"No, I don't think I'd better," the Orchid said sadly. "Wives don't seem to like me. They get jealous. We'll keep this to ourselves."

"Perhaps we'd better," I agreed and wondered what her game was.

TRIXIE SAW THE powder on my coat lapel when I came in the sitting room, and said acidly, "Necking?"

"With the Orchid. I wanted her to meet my dear little wife, Susan, but she begged off. Wives don't usually like her."

"*Susan?*" Trixie had fire in her eye. "I could skin you for that, Mike Harris! Why not Abigail to that hussy?"

"Why not? Susan Abigail it is."

I got the door locked just in time.

THOMPSON LONG DISTANCED from Washington in the morning.

"She's putting the screws on Maxwell," he crabbed over the wire. "Wants her dough quick, or else. The old man's frantic. He thought he'd have a couple of weeks yet anyway. Haven't you done anything?"

"It looks like I've done too much," I decided. "She wants Maxwell cleaned up before she cleans me."

"Well, get some action!" Thompson yelled. "If this thing goes sour on you, you're washed up with the Blaine Agency. It's that important."

"Button your lip," I advised. "They can hear you across the hall here. Tell Maxwell to put another padlock on his checkbook. No dame's going to toss a quarter of a million away by getting rash. He's safe enough as long as he stalls."

Thompson's groan traveled clear down from Washington. "I hope for your sake that's right," he warned.

And so did I. The Blaine Agency had a little trick of loading all the responsibility on the ones who drew a case, and then if they didn't come through, heads began to fall. It worked nine times out of ten. But Waldo Maxwell's quarter of a million and the Orchid were a big bite.

She was a wise one, dangerous as dynamite.

Trixie heard me out.

"You can't stall any longer, loud mouth," she decided. "Necking parties may be your forte, but you'll have to cut them short. I've been watching that hussy. She never speaks to anyone who might be in the racket with her. And a dime to a promise that those letters are not in her hotel room here. She wouldn't dare keep them so close."

"She has a maid."

"I've seen the maid!" Trixie snapped.

And so had I. A beauty, and a crook, if I knew my way around. "We've got to pull a fast one," I decided.

"He thinks," Trixie marveled. "Well, produce before we both get fired."

"I'm going swimming," I told her.

I MET THE Orchid on the beach, where she had said the night before she'd be. She wore black beach pajamas trimmed with white, and against her creamy skin they were enough to stop the breath and scuttle good resolutions. She gave me a smile to go with them. "Where is your wife?"

"Reading. No sunburn wanted."

"You poor neglected boy. It must be lonesome at times."

I held my breath until my face got red, and stuttered, "N-not when I'm with you." And we got along famously.

All the time I was wondering where she kept those letters of Maxwell's. Trixie was right. Not in her room. That would be the first place private dicks would look. And despite the fact that Trixie had seen no one with her, Thompson's hint that she did not work alone kept pricking at my mind.

So I admired the big diamond ring on her finger and told her about the jewels I had bought the little woman since the oil wells came in. Three hundred grand worth, diamonds, pearls, emeralds, and what not.

The Orchid swallowed the hook. "What a fortunate woman your wife is," she sighed. "I haven't seen her wearing any."

I grinned. "She's afraid to. Jewel thieves. So she keeps them in the bottom of her trunk."

The Orchid lay there on the sand like a lazy cat. Her pink finger nails dug in gently when I said that. I saw her leg muscles stiffen slightly. But she didn't bat an eye.

"How dangerous," she warned abruptly. "She should keep them in a safety deposit box."

"Susan doesn't think so," I yawned. "She likes to take them out and play with them. She's like a kid. Always wanted a diamond ring—and then got a lapful. And she's convinced no one would ever think of looking in the false bottom she had built into her trunk."

"I suppose she's right," the Orchid nodded lazily. "But just the same if they were mine I wouldn't take chances."

"Not you," I thought. Aloud I said: "Let's forget 'em. If she is robbed, I'll buy her some more. And how about taking a ride with me this evening? The wife is going to be downstairs playing bridge until late. I may have to leave tomorrow. Got a wire from my partner."

She looked at me through her lashes, smiling, mysterious, inscrutable. "Do you really want to?" she murmured.

"Try me," I dared.

"At eight," she said.

And I wondered whether I was being a fool after all. She looked soft and inviting as honey—and I knew she was dangerous as a cobra.

WALDO MAXWELL SAID harshly, "You are a fool!"

"I know I am," I agreed.

"We all act the fool now and then."

He winced, said something savagely under his breath and prowled back and forth. I had run him down in one of those fantastic villas that huddled up little narrow drives just off the beach. Simplicity by the hundred thousand dollars' worth. Handkerchief sized lawns, tile roofs, and luxury inside that would dim the Arabian nights.

It was indiscreet, I knew. I shouldn't have gone near him. But I needed action quick, and he was the only one who could give it to me. And there he prowled around the room like an enraged old bear, his dewlaps shaking, his white hair mussed where he had shoved his fingers through it, a scowl deepening the wrinkles over his rimless eyeglasses.

Waldo Maxwell might have been able to tame a multi-millionaire board of directors, but he had never tried Michael Harris of the Blaine Agency before. "Do I get it?" I demanded.

"It is an insane request!" he blurted violently.

"I know. I've thought it all over. If something isn't done quick, you're going to be splashed on the front pages, or out a quarter of a million," I reminded. "You haven't a thing on that dame. She's got you by your reputation and you can't even yip. Unless I'm wrong about the contents of those letters."

"No—no! I was out of my mind when I wrote them. Don't mention them! Are you certain you can control this insane—this plan of yours?"

I would have felt sorry for him, if I hadn't remembered he could sign his name to a check for five millions, and still have plenty left in the sock. "What would you give to have her come begging for mercy?" I asked.

Waldo Maxwell showed his teeth in a smile, gentle as a wolf's. "It would be some consolation for the humiliation I have been put to," he confessed.

"Then come through with what I need."

He glanced at a platinum cased watch and made up his

mind abruptly. "They will be delivered to your hotel some time before six," he promised.

"Can I count on that?"

"Young man, you heard me. Sometime before six."

So I left, satisfied.

And he came through.

I OPENED THE sealed brown paper package and poured the contents on the sitting room table. Trixie took one look and squealed: "Mike, where did you get these?"

"Kris Kringle," I grinned. "Now do you believe in fairies?"

"I've never seen such good looking imitations."

"I'll bet you never have," I agreed. "Not a phony among them? Every stone and setting is the real McCoy."

And I didn't blame Trixie for going pale and sick when she looked at me. That mess of diamond rings, bracelets, necklaces and whatnots needed a lot of explaining. Trixie picked up a pearl necklace and ran it through her fingers.

"Tell me, Mike," she commanded.

"Waldo Maxwell," I admitted. "It was like pulling eye teeth, but I got him to buy the lot on consignment. If they're returned, he gets his money back. If not—he'll probably have a heart seizure."

Trixie put her little hands on her little hips and looked me up and down with her lips pressed tightly together. "Have you gone insane, Mike Harris?"

"That has a familiar ring," I recalled. "Maxwell wanted to know the same thing."

"I think you have! What are you going to do with all this jewelry? Why, it—it must be worth a fortune."

"It is," I agreed. "And we're going to put it all in that little false bottom in your trunk, and you're going downstairs this evening and play bridge, and I'm sneaking off for an automobile ride with the Orchid."

"And leave all this up here?"

"Exactly."

Trixie bristled. "Now I know you're out of your mind! We'll do nothing of the sort! You can waste another evening making sheep's eyes at that cat if you care to, but I'm staying in and sit on this jewelry, or take it down to the hotel safe."

"Jealous?"

Trixie tossed her head. "Of you, big mouth?"

"We'll do as I say."

"If we do," Trixie snapped, "something tells me we are in for grief. I think that massive brain of yours is cracking under the strain.".

"Don't think," I advised. "It's dangerous."

IF I HAD stopped to think I would have gone shaky myself. For I knew what Waldo Maxwell and Trixie did not—that lot of jewelry was in greater danger than if I had tossed it on the lobby floor and walked off. It might have been returned from there. And I didn't dare use phonies. A slick crook would have spotted them the first look. So I shut my eyes and walked into the manager's office and asked for four young bellhops who could ride bicycles, keep their mouths shut, and stay honest for a twenty dollar bill.

He looked at me as if I were addled. "Of course, Mr. Blaine—I mean to say, we strive to furnish every service, but—"

"Then service me," I cut him off.

"I'm serious and in a hurry."

Grant the Palm Beach Palo Verde service. They delivered. I chased the manager out of his office, talked turkey
to those bellhops, and hung a hundred dollar prize up to
sweeten their twenties. All four of them could outthink
the average guest they roomed. In five minutes I drilled
them letter perfect, and they scattered with expense money.

THE ORCHID SIGHED dreamily. "Isn't the surf lovely?"

"Great," I agreed, and held her hand tighter while I
looked over to the beach.

Sure enough, there was a surf frothing in through the
moonlight. Pretty, too, if a fellow had time to look at it. I
didn't. My mind was on Trixie back there in the hotel playing bridge. And on my five bellhops, and the Orchid beside
me on the front seat of the big rented sedan. No chauffeur
this time. I didn't want to be bothered in case quick action
was needed.

But for the time being we had no action as we loafed
south in the moonlight with the open sea on the left. Some
night. Some scenery. Some girl. I forgot the times I had
called myself a fool for throwing in with the Blaine Agency.
Nights when the rain ran down my neck, and guns barked
out of the blackness. Days when nerves were worn to a
frazzle matching wits with the smartest crooks in the country. A dog's life, until I met the moon and the sea, and
the Orchid went limp inside my arms as we loafed along
through the miles. She was concentrated forgetfulness in
a gorgeous shell.

Only I didn't forget. When I wrap my arm around a
snake I watch it. I tested her out. "We'd better be getting
back, beautiful."

"Not yet," she sighed, and came over another inch. "It's so lovely out here tonight. I could drive until morning."

"You won't, sister," I thought—and gave her three miles more before I turned and stepped on the gas.

"You are driving too fast," the Orchid protested.

I patted her knee. "I'm a fast chap."

"You're a fresh one," she said, and tried to steer me over to Lake Worth and down through West Palm Beach, stalling for time.

"Little girls shouldn't be out so late," I stalled back. "I have a headache, and I'm going to turn in. I'll stay over another day and we'll take this up tomorrow night."

"But I will not be free tomorrow night."

"My loss," I mourned, and rolled her back to the hotel far faster than she had gone away from it.

The Orchid said good night without much graciousness and went in the front entrance. When I parked the car one of the four bellhops popped out of the night. His eyes were wide with suppressed excitement.

"Your room was entered, Mr. Blaine!" he said breathlessly. "A thin man with a black mustache. About twenty minutes ago."

"Any trouble? Where are the others?"

"They haven't come back yet. I've been waiting here for you."

"Be back in a few minutes," I told him, and hurried inside, lifted Trixie from her bridge game and took her up to the suite.

"Powder on your coat again," Trixie sniffed while I unlocked the door. "I'm getting sick of a half baked Romeo underfoot all the time."

"It's my charm," I grinned.

"It's your oil wells!" Trixie snapped as she marched into the room.

She beat me to the trunk while I was closing the door. And a moment later pulled her hand out of the hidden compartment in the bottom and whirled on me.

"They're gone! Every stone and setting; while you played the fool and I play bridge like you ordered! Oh, why did Thompson ever put an idiot like you on this?" She stamped her foot, grabbed my arm and shook it. "Say something! Don't stand there grinning like an idiot! They're gone, I tell you!"

"That's great," I said heartily. And Trixie almost swooned.

While she was getting her breath back I came out of my room sliding a clip into my automatic. "Hat and coat," I directed. "We're going out."

"Where?"

"Ask me something I know. It's a great night."

AND TRIXIE ALMOST swooned again. But she was ready in sixty seconds, slipping a small edition of my automatic in her purse. Tucked away somewhere, too, was a fountain pen gas gun. Trixie never went without it.

A second bellhop was waiting when we got outside, his bicycle tipped on the grass. "What luck?" I asked him, and held my breath for the answer. It might mean the end of Waldo Maxwell's diamonds and pearls. If it did, it was my finish.

"Over in West Palm Beach," he said quickly. "Two of the boys are watching."

"Get in the back," I ordered.

"We'll talk as we drive."

"Who are they?" Trixie demanded as we all tumbled in.

"Bellhops."

"It doesn't make sense."

"Nothing does." And as I drove, the boys in the back seat talked fast. One of them had been in an empty room where he could watch the door of our suite; another outside covering the windows; and the other two had been downstairs near a telephone.

There had been no second story work. A well dressed man had walked down the hall, fitted a key into the door of our suite, stepped inside, remained a few minutes, and stepped out again, natural and easy. He had walked out of the hotel into a waiting car—and three bellhops had jumped on waiting bicycles and followed. Simple as that.

"And you didn't tell them to call the house detective?" Trixie asked thinly.

"Think of the publicity, my dear."

"I think you are a reckless idiot!" Trixie flared.

"You've called me that before," I reminded. "He who steals and runs away will surely pay some other day."

"Mad!" Trixie muttered despairingly. "Stark, raving mad!"

Cross west on the brightly lighted bridge over Lake Worth and you come into another world. The coast highway runs through West Palm Beach, and now and then a tourist stops off and settles. Apartment buildings, cottages, cozy houses—it was like getting home from phantasy land. We found the other two bellhops beside their bikes at a corner in the residential section.

Their dope was short and sweet. The car they had

followed had turned into a driveway in the middle of the block, and was still in there.

"Stay here with the car," I said to Trixie.

And she said: "Never again. You need someone with sense to watch you."

"Meaning a woman," I said sarcastically. "Nevertheless, you stay here. This isn't a tea party."

So she stayed, and two of the bellhops walked down one side of the street and the other guided me to the one story stucco cottage where Waldo Maxwell's jewels had flitted. One side room was lighted. The window shades were down.

I sent the kid across the street and walked to the back of the house. A big car was standing in the driveway, heading toward the street.

No one was worried inside—and why should they be, after strolling out of the Palo Verde so easily? A radio was playing jazz. The screen door on the back porch was unlocked, and so was the kitchen door. I pulled my automatic as I stepped inside.

A swinging door opened out of the kitchen, a hall beyond that, and to the left was an archway into a dining room. A voice said: "God, Harry, this bracelet ought to be worth five grand anyway. The emerald is good for two, and most of the diamonds will bulge a carat and a half."

And a second voice, "Shall we split his necklace and peddle the pearls separate?"

"I wouldn't," I advised as I stepped in. "That's a sucker trick."

There were two of them, sleek, good looking young fellows. One knocked over a chair as he jumped back and reached under his coat. When he saw my gun he stood still.

Waldo Maxwell's bait was spread over the table. They hadn't been able to keep their hands off it. Harry had a little black mustache that jerked as he got out: "What are you doing here?"

"Don't be so formal," I said. "This is a pinch."

And Harry gasped, "It's a frame? He talks like a dick!"

"You mind reader," I said. "He is a dick. Turn around while I collect your rods, suckers."

Harry took a chance, dodged and grabbed for his gun. I shot him through the shoulder. The next instant the light went out as his sidekick reached the wall switch. They both cut loose as I dropped to the floor behind the table. Four shots that were almost one—and a door slammed....

I was alone with my ears ringing and the radio blaring away in the next room.

That was what slowed me up! My ears and the radio. I couldn't hear their movements, had to go slow for fear they were waiting for me. The motor in the driveway suddenly spun. Gears whined as it rushed toward the street.

And just as I opened the front door there was a terrific crash at the street. They had run into another car in front of the driveway as they turned sharp to avoid it.

I ran out.

Two groping, stumbling figures reeled on the sidewalk, fighting at their eyes. I backed away quick from the thin drifting vapor they were trying to escape.

It was my rented car they had run into. Trixie joined me, and said coolly: "I drove up when I heard the shots, and blocked them. I let them have the gas through the open window of their car."

"Good girl!" I yelled. "Tell those bellhops to collar 'em

until the cops get here!" And I ran back into the house while the neighbors poured out into the street.

I reached the street again just as the police car slid up. We settled the rest in the station house. It took the jewels on the dining room table, the testimony of the bellhops, our credentials and a telephone call to Waldo Maxwell to clear Trixie and me enough so we could leave for the evening.

And at that we were told it was damn queer business, and there was going to be a lot of explaining before the matter was settled.

"There will be," I promised.

Trixie was wild as a taxi took us back to the Palo Verde.

"See what you've done with that idiotic jewelry!" she stormed. "A man shot, two cars wrecked, serious charges plastered everywhere—with all the publicity it will bring—and Maxwell is as bad off as ever!"

"We'll ask the Orchid about that," I said.

TRIXIE WAS STILL breathing hard when I knocked on the Orchid's door. The maid, almost as good looking as the Orchid, answered it. She took one look at Trixie and informed us that Miss Dean had retired.

"Too bad," I regretted. "Get her up." And I pushed on in.

The Orchid met us in a frothy negligee that was enough to stop the breath. "What does this mean?" Her voice was knife-edged.

"Harry and his sidekick are in the West Palm Beach police station," I told her. "They were caught with the jewelry. It belonged to Waldo Maxwell."

I saw the maid, standing in the doorway, turn pale and

press a hand against her throat. But the Orchid's eyes began to blaze past her long lashes.

"So you tricked me!" she said through her teeth.

"Gloria," I sighed, "it broke my heart to do it. But you've been loose long enough."

"Waldo Maxwell is behind this!"

"Sad—but so."

I've seen a furious tigress behind the bars. But never have I been so close to one. The Orchid's face turned marble white. Her eyes narrowed to points.

"Maxwell won't get away with this!" she blazed. "I'll spread his name over every paper in the country! Tell him he'd better run here and settle it quick! If those men aren't out by tomorrow, I'll call the reporters in and give them the story of their lives!"

"Can you back it up?"

"Certainly! I have letters!"

"You had," I corrected. "What do you think I planted that jewelry for? I wanted to uncover your boy friends who were probably holding Maxwell's letters. I found them in the bottom of a suitcase in their house. You might call Maxwell from the police station tonight and ask him for a little mercy. He's got an answer all ready."

She spat at me like a cat.

Trixie said later that gave her hope for me.

DEATH TAKES PASSAGE

The Yacht Stardust *Had Become a Ship of
Murder on Which Men Fought for Some
Unknown and Mysterious Reason*

1

THE MISSING EMBEZZLER

SIMPSON, IN THE Blaine Agency office in Miami, had a fat middle, a bald spot, and nose-glasses. Simpson strutted when he walked, reminded me of a fussy professor in a ladies' seminary—and talked like a longshoreman. No better man ever snapped cuffs on a crook—but then the Blaine Agency hired no sour ones.

So I listened when Simpson adjusted those prim nose-glasses, folded his hands across the bulge in his waistline and swore: "Dammit, Mike Harris, I'm glad they sent you down here! Hell's bells and little horse flies! I'm up a tree!"

It was like hearing a deacon let go at Sunday school. I had to grin as I wise cracked back: "Dat ole debbil underworld clawing at your britches, huh? What's the moan?"

Simpson plucked a stogy out of his breast pocket, chewed off the end and scratched a match under the edge of his desk. The ghost of a sour grin went across his mouth as he puffed hard and looked at me.

"They tell me you're the hardest case in the whole Blaine organization," Simpson grunted. "Three pints of hell and kummel under that red hair."

I accepted modestly. "Thanks for the cake. We've got

Daly staggered, uttered a choking scream. His
hands made a fluttery lift to his throat...

another who makes me look like an old softy, but let it go. What's your sad story?"

"It isn't exactly sad," Simpson confessed.

"They always are when I get 'em," I gave Simpson, a trifle sour myself. I was still grouching from having been shot down here to Miami when I had been planning on a little Times Square and hi-de-ho.

"Ever hear of Anton McSwiggin?" Simpson asked me.

"No," said I, "and lived to be twenty-nine in the meantime. Who is Anton McSwiggin, and why?"

"Anton McSwiggin," said Simpson, "seems to be a rich man."

"Is that all?" I gave him. "Since when has it been a crime to be rich? He's merely unlucky. Where's he been hiding the last three years?"

But Simpson couldn't raise another smile for me. He scowled at the end of his stogy again.

"Anton McSwiggin," he said solemnly, "owns a yacht. The *Stardust*. Ninety-one feet long. Diesel engines. All steel hull and ocean going lines."

"Interesting, if true," I sighed. "You forgot the color of the paint and the length of the sheets—but let it pass. I'm almost beginning to believe you're interested in this yacht."

"In Anton McSwiggin," Simpson corrected fussily. "In how he got the money to buy that yacht, not to speak of what he intends to do with it."

"Is that all?" I said weakly.

Simpson had me stalled. Here I'd come down to Miami looking for a big case, and he was talking yacht specifications. Anton McSwiggin sounded like the usual run of millionaires who cluttered up the Florida east coast from December to May. Most of them respectable—legally so anyway. Not a crook's mug in a harborful.

"It's enough!" Simpson snapped.

"Bootleg?" I suggested hopefully. "Drugs? Alien running…."

"Rum running isn't fashionable any more," Simpson corrected. "Miami isn't a dope port and all the aliens are running back to Europe, where they can eat. This is a big thing. And delicate, Harris, delicate."

"My touch is delicate and my discretion deadly."

"Ever hear of Roger Caldwell?" Simpson asked.

I had to shake my head. "Never did."

"He was vice-president and treasurer of the United Service Insurance Company of Louisville, Kentucky. A fat and flourishing outfit doing business all through the Middle West."

I lifted an eyebrows *"Was* vice-president?"

"Yes. He left a shortage of eight hundred and seventy-five thousand dollars in his accounts, mostly United States government bonds and cash. He cleaned out their liquid reserve."

I whistled. "He wasn't a piker anyway. What'd he do with it? Stock market?"

"No," said Simpson. "Caldwell never played the market, gambled or chased women. He was a conservative bachelor. Two months ago, when the annual audit was completed, his accounts were in perfect shape. He'd been with the company fourteen years, and not a breath of suspicion against him. It was a job that had been planned for a long time. Every move thought out. When the time was ripe he packed up and vanished."

"But what," I asked, "has that got to do with Anton McSwiggin and his ninety-one foot yacht?"

Simpson wouldn't be hurried.

"The insurance company retained the Blaine Agency at once," Simpson said. "All government passport agencies were notified and outgoing boats watched. Europe, Central America and Canada have been circularized. And nary a trace of Roger Caldwell. He simply dropped out of sight. We're convinced he's lying low in this country, waiting for the right moment to make a break. He's smart enough to know he can't stay long and not be caught."

"Eight hundred and seventy-five thousand dollars will take him a long way."

"Perhaps," said Simpson. "We've investigated him back

to childhood and established that he has a half brother who has a police record in Philadelphia and Chicago under the alias of Peter Lewis. Bank robbery, liquor running and racketeering. Peter Lewis disappeared from Chicago a month before Roger Caldwell looted the United Service Company."

"Both in it, eh? But still I don't see where Anton McSwiggin's yacht figures in."

"McSwiggin bought that yacht about four weeks ago, from a firm of yacht brokers in New York," Simpson told me. "She was laid up here for the season and McSwiggin outfitted her hurriedly for a long cruise. McSwiggin is from Chicago. Has a police record there, although we can't connect him with Pete Lewis."

I got it then.

"So you think Anton McSwiggin may know something about Roger Caldwell and the eight hundred and seventy-five grand," I guessed.

Simpson blinked at me through his glasses and pulled on his stogy.

"We're curious," he admitted. "There's no proof. But we can't see why Anton McSwiggin should suddenly buy a yacht and decide to take a long trip. He can't be stopped. He's within his rights as a citizen. But when the *Stardust* sails from Miami we want to know where she goes and what she does. You're elected. Know anything about seamanship?"

"A little."

"So much the better," Simpson nodded. "McSwiggin has the reputation of being a hard customer. He might make trouble if you go to sea without knowing anything about your job."

"Perfectly all right with the Blaine Agency, of course. Anything else?"

"I guess not," Simpson said as calmly as if he had just handed an invitation to a fish fry. "You'll need some seagoing clothes—and a gun. Go to the address on this card. McSwiggin's captain has made inquiries there about a crew. You'll be included. As soon as the *Stardust* puts to sea you're on your own."

IT LOOKED LIKE a wild goose chase, but I was used to that, too. A deep sea cruise on a private yacht might not be so bad after all. I put Mike Harris, red headed dick, in cold storage and turned salty. A couple of hours shopping on Flagler Street gave me two cheap suitcases and a seagoing outfit.

The address Simpson had given me was an employment agency.

And at ten-thirty the next morning I met Captain Krupp of the *Stardust*. Captain Krupp may have been a real captain and he may not. He looked a hard case, stocky, strong, with a square face and a brassy, lifeless stare. Booze had put red veins in his nose, and he used snuff.

"I don't know where we're going or how long we'll be out," he told me. "You'll sign for six months, no questions asked. Duties to be anything assigned to you."

"Good enough," I agreed.

Captain Krupp opened a round box of snuff, tucked a pinch of it under his lip, and gave me that brassy lifeless stare.

"You look like a smart young fellow," he growled.

"I led my class in the eighth grade, Captain," I said, with a nautical hitch to my belt.

The captain half closed one eye—and it wasn't a wink. I got to know that look later, and there was a time to come when it would put cold shivers down my back. "See if you're smart enough to keep your mouth shut about this trip," he growled again, and left me.

The *Stardust* was a trim little yacht—a beauty. Snow white with blue funnels and trimmings. It was easy to believe her former owner had hated to sell. The crew bunked forward, and I got my first shock as we sat down for supper. They were a hard cased lot. Captain Krupp must have combed half the dives in Miami for them. They hogged down that supper like they hadn't had a square meal in a year; and every man looked like he would enjoy a fight with his neighbor.

Supplies had been coming aboard all day, and next morning they continued. The lot of us turned to help stow them away. Bags, sacks, crates, canned goods and fresh goods. We put enough fresh meat in the refrigerators to feed a regiment.

I took it all in. What kind of a trip was this planned to be? Six months and no questions asked—and enough food to last a year. No one seemed to know any more than I did, or if so kept their mouths shut.

During the morning Anton McSwiggin, owner, was in evidence, talking with Captain Krupp. He was a tall bag of bones, spare as a fence rail, with a long, bony, angular face, and big knobby wrists and hands. A queer one. His nose hooked over his tight mouth like a vulture's beak. But it was his stare that got me. He seemed to be looking for something all the time, here, there, everywhere. And when he saw you he didn't see you. There was something queer about him. I sensed it, but couldn't put my finger on it.

Along in the afternoon four passengers arrived; two women and a man, coming aboard at different times. And I perked up at sight of the women. I could have spotted their type with one eye closed and the other astigmatic. I've fed bubble juice to too many girlies to go wrong on them. Not one of the three was over twenty-five. They all could have made the front row in the chorus; high fliers and fast steppers, and they came aboard that yacht looking like they'd never seen one before outside a picture page.

But it was the man, with his taxi load of shiny new luggage, who made me smell something sour. He was a slim young fellow in his late twenties, dressed like a tailor's ad, with a walk that swaggered. One look and I ticketed him. He was a sport, a fast worker, a smart customer. His kind had no more business on a yacht than a debutante in an old ladies' home.

And then, late that afternoon, I got a shock that almost made me drop the case of canned peaches I had taken off the truck backed up there on the dock. A taxi had rolled up and stopped. A little slip of a girl got out, handed the driver a bill, took her change and watched him unload three pieces of cheap luggage.

It was Trixie Meehan. And lest you go wrong, Trixie Meehan was the best woman operator the Blaine Agency ever put on the payroll. She was a frail little thing, with flowery eyes, a face that would have taken prizes in any beauty contest, and a wistful, helpless manner that made big strong men grow ambitious and protective.

And behind all that Trixie had a tongue with the bite of an asp, muscles better than most men's, and a brain that was fearful and deadly. Trixie was the hardest case in the whole Blaine organization. We were always running across each other—and she usually had her knife out for me.

I set the case of peaches down with a thump and walked over to her.

"Madame," says I, for the benefit of the driver, "can I take your bags aboard for you?" And under my breath I snarled, "What the blazes are you doing here?"

"Yes, driver, that will be all," Trixie murmured sweetly. "This man says he will help me." And as the driver climbed back behind his wheel, Trixie hissed under her breath: "Don't stand there gawking like a baboon, Mike Harris! Pick up a couple of these bags and look intelligent, if it's in you."

"Lay off the wise cracks!" I snapped, picking up two of her bags. "What are you doing down here? I thought you had gone to New York."

"I'm the new stewardess," Trixie said sweetly. "They called me back to keep an eye on you, I think. My name is Gertrude Smith, and I never saw you before." Trixie gave me a judicial glance, dirty overalls, hands and everything. "And I don't think I'd want to," she added.

Simpson hadn't told me the agency was figuring on sending anyone else along, let alone Trixie Meehan. I think I'd have taken the first train back to New York if he had.

I got in Trixie's way as she turned toward the gangplank with the third bag.

"Listen," I said, "this yacht ain't no place for you. It

doesn't look right to me—besides, I can't stand being so close to you for more than a day or two."

"Out of my way, Ape!" Trixie said pleasantly. "I don't like it any more than you do, but I'm a woikin' goil, and I'm willing to endure even you. Get those bags aboard before someone gets wise that you're making a stupid play."

And there was nothing to do but go along with her. As we reached the gangplank, Trixie hissed: "Stop mumbling under your breath. Someone will hear you and know you haven't good sense."

And just then I looked up and caught Captain Krupp's eye on me. "Yes, madam," I said politely, and let Trixie sail ahead.

2

BOSS OF THE SCULLERY

THE WORD WAS passed around we'd sail in the morning. And shortly after we'd finished eating that evening the captain sent for me. He was in his cabin, with a half empty quart of liquor beside him and his face flushed to the color of a ripe beet.

"Harris," he said thickly, "did you ever wait on table?"

"Sure," I said, taking it blind. "I'm a swell waiter."

"Good. A damn cabin steward I hired got himself run down by an automobile this evening. You'll bunk with the cook and draw white coats from him. Watch your manners while you're waiting on the passengers."

"Yes, sir," says I—and really meant it. This was just the break I had been waiting for. I moved back with the cook right away.

Karmos was the cook's name, a stocky Greek with a flat scowling face, and none too glad to see me in our cramped little cabin.

"Get seasick and I'll make it hot for you," he started off our friendship. "We're short handed and I won't have time to do anything for you."

I grinned, instead of picking a fight. "Never got seasick in my life," I lied. "Where are we going?"

Karmos shrugged out of a stained white coat and slammed it in his lower berth.

"I don't know and I don't give a damn!" he snapped. "The fewer questions you ask the better it'll be for you, redhead. There's a buzzer in your pantry off the galley, and one there on the wall. You stick close to them, jump when you're called, and keep your nose out of everything else."

It was going to be hard to keep my temper. The more I saw of the job the less I liked it. But my curiosity was growing. Everywhere I turned I ran into a suspicious wall of mystery. Karmos might have been a cook, but he didn't look like a seagoing man to me.

I played steward all evening, scampering between my steward's pantry and the big social cabin amidships. It was trimmed with teak, mahogany and tapestry, decorated by a man who knew his business, for people with good taste. And the more drinks I mixed, brought, poured, the more certain I became that evening that everything was not on the up and up.

The ladies had never met before—and seemed perfect strangers to Anton McSwiggin, the owner. Shields, the slim, dapper young fellow with the swaggering walk, didn't say anything that made it look like he had met Anton McSwiggin either. The pantry had a liquor stock that would have put a speakeasy to shame; but all those three Broadway fuzzies could pronounce was champagne. How they loved it! Pickings must have been hard up north, and they were making up for lost time.

They chattered of this and that, pulled the grand lady act, and then let loose a few squeals as champagne warmed them up.

Shields drank a bottle with them, but I noticed he took it slow, and looked bored behind his laughs. A smart customer, this Shields.

Anton McSwiggin slouched down in a high backed chair covered with red leather, and now and then sipped a little Napoleon brandy he had asked me to bring. His bony, angular face was solemn, almost forbidding. With those knobby, red skinned wrists and hands he looked like a big farmer all dressed up with a yacht and no place to go. But every time I saw his eyes they were moving quickly about, looking, but hardly paying any attention to what was going on in the cabin. He looked queerer than ever to me.

I bumped into Trixie. She was tricked out in a stewardess's white outfit, coming out of a cabin with a pile of towels over one arm. She took one look at my white coat and silver tray, and simpered: "So you're in service too, Ape?"

"Dry up," I said, "What do you think of it?"

"I don't think, Big Brain; I've been too busy making beds. But I'll say one thing—I never saw three sweeter tarts chiselling at a bank roll. Who have they got their delicate little claws hooked for?"

"McSwiggin?"

"Don't be painful. That horsefaced length of gristle never thought about a woman in his life. He hasn't got an extra pulse beat in his wrist, and I'll bet he keeps his money pinned in his pants with a safety pin."

"They aren't bringing hoity-toit along to entertain the crew," I muttered. "That only leaves Shields, and he looks like a live wire. He may be a softhead for dames, but I can't spot him three and make it look reasonable."

"I haven't heard him speak Turkish," Trixie assented. "There's a nigger in the woodpile, or little Trixie never saw a Tom show. Wind up your massive brain, Sherlock, and pull the answer out of your sleeve."

"*Steward!* Hurry up with that ice!" one of the dames shrilled from the saloon.

"If you knew how silly you look in that white coat…" Trixie simpered.

"Go tear a sheet!" I snarled, and stalked off to my pantry. Trixie could get under my hide in thirty seconds.

WE SAILED AT midnight, without any warning—just like that. Lines aboard, Captain Krupp at the wheel, and Biscayne Bay dropping astern as we headed out through the channel toward the open sea. Krupp must have known his way about; there was no trouble about it.

And the radio was going hot-cha by then, and all three of the girls were bosom friends. I noticed Anton McSwiggin up in the wheelhouse with Captain Krupp, dour, solemn.

The sparkle and glitter of Miami Beach fell behind in the northwest as the *Stardust* rolled easily through the swells of the Gulf Stream. We dropped astern the lighthouse on the shoals west of the south entrance to the Bay, and had the Atlantic to ourselves for a time. The whoopla ladies staggered off to bed. The crew, except for the night watch, had already turned in. I went off duty dead tired, wondering where Trixie and I were going to end up—and what all this had to do with Roger Caldwell and the eight hundred and seventy-five grand he had copped from the insurance company. He wasn't aboard, I was certain.

KARMOS WASN'T IN our little two-by-four cabin as I shucked my white coat. I was dead tired, but not sleepy.

I started on deck for a cigarette and some fresh air; and as I passed the end of the short corridor leading past the starboard cabins I saw Karmos just turning toward me. I could have sworn he had just come out of Shields' cabin. He scowled and caught up with me out on deck.

"I thought you were forward," I said, lighting a cigarette.

The yellow flare of the match showed Karmos' flat face, sullen and angry. His thick hand grabbed my arm as I turned to the rail, swinging me back.

"What the hell d'you mean spying on me?" he flared.

I slapped his hand off, and marked him down for a strong one by his grip. How strong I had yet to find out.

"Don't paw me!" I snapped. "I wasn't spying on you— and why should I?"

"I seen you layin' low at the end of that corridor!"

"If I had been, you wouldn't have seen me," I gave him. "What business is it of mine if you're back in the saloon? The passengers have turned in. If you can get by with it you're that much ahead."

Karmos was quiet a moment. I could feel his manner change. A sly note crept in his voice. He must have thought he was a crafty one, or I was a fool.

"I thought I'd go back and get a fistful of cigarettes," he said. "Maybe I made you wrong, kid. Here, have one. They're better'n we can afford."

He sounded like a Chicago hoodlum. The cigarette he handed me was straw tipped, Turkish tobacco. There had been several boxes of them on the saloon table that evening.

"Thanks," I said, slipping my cheap one away and lighting it. "I was thinking about getting a fistful myself. You out-thought me."

Karmos caught me on the shoulder.

"I'll out-think you every time, kid. Let me do the thinkin' for us both, and we'll live like kings. Goin' to turn in now?"

"I'll stay up a little while," I decided. "I'm never sleepy the first night out."

I must have been there at the rail half an hour, perhaps longer, watching the green blobs of phosphorescent light swirling away from the trim hull of the yacht. The Diesel engine was throbbing steadily down below, the exhaust patting in a soft monotone from the single stack. Deck lights had been turned out. The coast was out of sight. I crossed over to the port side and watched a big liner rush up from the south, pass half a mile away, steaming towards New York. This stretch of the Gulf Stream along the south Florida coast was like a boulevard, ships passing up and down all the time.

Karmos stuck in my mind. He might have been back in the saloon—the cigarette he had given me looked like it—but he hadn't been coming from there when I saw him. I would have bet a month's pay against a nickel cigar he had been in Shields' cabin. But what had the ship's cook been doing in a passenger's cabin at that hour of the night? It didn't make sense. And why had Karmos flared into rage when aware that I had seen him?

I was trying to untangle that bit of mystery when it happened—a shrill scream of terror smashing the peace of the night. A woman's scream, somewhere on the starboard side. I threw my cigarette over the rail and ran toward it.

For a moment when I got in that starboard passageway I thought I might have been mistaken. It was quiet, peaceful, dimly lighted and deserted—and then the nearest door flung open and one of the girls stepped out, wrapped in a frilly negligee. Her eyes were wide, startled. Surprise and fear had ruined her *grande dame* manner. Her name was Gladys Ward, a smoky-eyed brunette, and at sight of me she cried shrilly: "What was that scream, steward? It—it woke me up."

"Lady," I said truthfully, "I don't know. Where was it?"

"How the devil do I know?" she snapped. "I don't think in my sleep!"

And then I saw it—one slim white hand projecting from the doorway of Shields' cabin, two doors farther along. I jumped to it, swearing under my breath. There it lay on the floor, limp, lax, a woman's hand in a cabin where she had no business to be. The door was ajar about a foot, no light inside.

I tried to shove it open, and her body blocked it. The brunette had followed me fearfully, was babbling half-hysterically: "What is it? W-what has happened? I knew it was something terrible—"

I ignored her, squeezed in through the door, watching my feet, and snapped on the light switch.

There she lay—a tall, stately blonde whose name had come to me that evening as Frances Lawes. Miss Lawes, of course; they were all misses, no matter what secrets the records held. She was dressed in the same dark blue traveling outfit she had worn that evening. Paint and rouge on lips and cheeks looked unnatural against her bloodless pallor. She lay in a crumpled heap, one arm out-thrust through the doorway, the other before her face.

3

DEATH BY A DAGGER

SHE WAS THE first thing in the cabin I saw. And I thought her dead. Then I saw Shields, and got another shock. He was crumpled back on his bunk, one leg hanging over to the floor, his face turned up to the ceiling and his arms lying limp and unnatural by his side. His eyes were open, the pupils rolled up almost out of sight. I had seen too many men like that to go wrong. It didn't need the slender bone haft of a stiletto sticking up over Shields' heart to tell me that he was dead.

By that time there was a stir of movement, an increasing babble of voices outside in the passageway as one of the other girls stumbled out of her cabin. I ignored all of them. Shields was in his shirt sleeves. The white linen cloth around the stiletto blade had been turned to an irregular crimson splotch. I guessed that Shields had been standing up when that stiletto had been buried to the hilt with terrific force. He had collapsed back against his bunk, dying quickly; and the killer had eased him back as he now lay.

The scream I had heard was explained too. I checked it by feeling Miss Lawes' pulse. It was faint, but steady. She had entered the cabin, discovered Shields, screamed and fainted.

I turned for a glass of water, thinking of Karmos, my flat-faced roommate. I knew now there had been no mistake about seeing him come out of this cabin. Shields' wrist was still warm, but cooling fast. He might have been dead three-quarters of an hour, an hour; it would be hard to say without expert medical testimony. Had he been dead then, or had Karmos killed him?

That funny exhibition of anger and crafty effort to cover it stuck in my mind as I flipped water in Miss Lawes' face. Did that gruesome sight on the bunk explain it? It was a lot easier to admit stealing cigarettes than to face a murder charge.

Miss Lawes gasped, sighed, opened her eyes, and suddenly shuddered as her head turned toward the bunk. But there were no more hysterics. She caught her lower lip between her teeth so hard I thought the blood would come, but remained silent as I lifted her to her feet.

"What happened?" I demanded.

The two girls out in the hall shoved the door open, were staring inside in fearful fascination. Miss Lawes looked at them. Her face hardened slightly. She drew a deep shuddering breath—and abruptly was in full control of herself.

"I don't know," she denied. "I wanted to speak to Mr. Shields. The door was unlocked so I stepped inside."

Just then Trixie, cool and competent in her white uniform, came to the door. She took one look and entered. "Something wrong?" she asked calmly. Chilled steel nerves Trixie had; you couldn't shake her.

"Only a little murder," I said sarcastically, and turned my attention to Miss Lawes. "You didn't turn the light on?"

She had straightened her dress, patted her blond hair

mechanically. There was a beautiful hard competence about her, a certain wariness in the appraising look she shot me from under her long lashes.

"I thought Mr. Shields was out," she explained in a low voice. "I was going to sit down on his bunk and wait for him in the darkness. And I put my hand on his chest, against the knife and blood." She shuddered, looked at the fingers of her left hand. They were stained faintly red. She scrubbed them against her skirt with a sudden panicky motion.

Trixie looked at the bunk, at me. "Who did this?"

"If I knew," I said sarcastically, "I'd ask him not to do it again. Go and notify the captain. This is his business."

Trixie could take orders when necessary. She left the cabin without argument, and she was hardly out of sight when I heard Captain Krupp's gruff voice down the hall. A moment later he shoved in through the doorway, followed by the tall, spare figure of Anton McSwiggin. Krupp swore at the sight, turned on me like a red-faced bull.

"Who killed this man?"

I denied knowledge, explained what had happened.

ANTON MCSWIGGIN LISTENED, pulling at his lower lip. His eyes slid here, there about the cabin, running over Shields' body, Miss Lawes, myself. And yet somehow I felt he wasn't paying much attention to the murder. He was listening though. When I finished he looked at Miss Lawes, asked softly:

"What were you doing here in Mr. Shields' cabin, Miss Lawes?"

He looked more like a vulture than ever as he murmured that; and the very quietness, mildness of his voice made it worse than ever. He reminded me of a vulture plucking leisurely, confidently, into a heap of carrion.

One of the girls out in the hall snickered. Miss Lawes flashed a look of dislike through the doorway and then braced her shoulders. I saw the muscles in her neck tighten, as if calling on hidden strength.

"I couldn't sleep," she explained steadily. "I wanted to talk to—to him—" Her glance barely indicated the body.

Anton McSwiggin lifted his eyebrows. "At this hour of the night?"

Captain Krupp's brassy stare accused her.

"Sounds funny!" he growled.

Miss Lawes plucked unsteadily at a dress button, but her voice remained firm. "Perhaps—but I didn't do this. Think a little harder, Captain."

"What d'you mean?" Krupp blustered.

Anton McSwiggin's knobby, red hand gestured him quiet. McSwiggin's stare wandered, stopped on me.

"You were on deck when Miss Lawes screamed, steward?"

"Yes."

"How long were you out there?"

"About an hour."

"You saw nothing, heard nothing suspicious?"

I hesitated, stopped. This was the parting of the ways. I thought I knew who had killed Shields. Certainly not this striking blonde beside me.

Anton McSwiggin was looking at me fixedly. A veil seemed to cover his eyes. His face was expressionless.

I said: "No—Miss Lawes' scream was the first I heard," before I quite knew why I did it.

"I see," said Anton McSwiggin noncommittally. His gaze wandered over all of us. "Have any of you seen this knife before?" He pointed at Shields' chest.

No one had.

McSwiggin pulled at his lower lip, sighed audibly.

"A ghastly piece of business," he murmured. "Sam Shields was a fine young man. I'm shocked, grieved. We shall miss him."

Miss Lawes asked the question I was thinking. "Are you going to take him back to Miami?"

Captain Krupp looked quickly at his owner. McSwiggin shook his head.

"We are on the high seas beyond the three mile limit. We can gain nothing by returning. We'll bury him here at sea."

Miss Lawes was pale, determined.

"I want to go back."

McSwiggin's vague gaze centered on her.

"Go to your cabin," he suggested in what was almost an order. "Captain Krupp, arrange for an immediate burial. The weather is warm. Waiting will do no good."

"Yes, sir."

Anton McSwiggin stepped through the door, saying to the girls in the passageway: "You two get to bed also. Stewardess!"

He jerked his head down the passageway.

Trixie went out without a word.

Captain Krupp snapped at me: "You're not needed here any more, steward."

And I went with the feeling that, whether needed or not, I wasn't wanted. It looked like a good time to keep my mouth shut, and eyes and ears open. We carried no wireless sending set. There was nothing to do but wait and look for the answer to Shields' death.

Karmos was asleep, snoring heavily, when I stepped into the cabin.

THEY BURIED SHIELDS at sea that night. I heard them—muffled activity, furtive voices, and finally through the open porthole of our cramped little cabin, Captain Krupp's hoarse command:

"Heave him over!"

And the shark filled waters of the Gulf Stream took Shields without prayer or ceremony. It was a heartless, callous thing to do. I slept fitfully the rest of the night—and Karmos snored.

Morning brought a warm sun, a sea like shimmering turquoise, and no land in sight. But I knew by the course we were laying, roughly southwest, that beyond that western horizon line were the Florida keys, stretching in a great arc down to Key West. We were heading toward Cuba, the Caribbean or the Gulf of Mexico—God knew where.

Karmos woke me getting up. I gave him the news. He paused, one leg in his trousers, bracing against the slight roll of the yacht, and stared at me with dropping jaw and paling face.

"Shields dead?" he choked.

"Murder," says I, getting down.

The Greek's swart face turned almost gray. If ever fear struck a man it got him then. "Who did it?" he asked hoarsely.

"Search me," I yawned. "Miss Lawes found him with a stiletto stuck in his heart. They buried him over the side last night."

Karmos belted his trousers, watching me. He started to speak, and swallowed his tongue. Blood crept back in his gray face, but he was still scared. He muttered as I quickly dressed, *"Threw him to the sharks...."*

And that was all.

Karmos was jumpy all morning. He looked guilty. Had he killed Shields, I wondered? If so, why?

Karmos wasn't the only queer one. It was a thin breakfast. Krupp wolfed his food noncommittally. Anton McSwiggin looked more like a vulture than ever as he ate silently. The girls straggled in late, and minced at their food, obviously uneasy.

Krupp was captain and stood a watch of his own. McSwiggin was standing a mate's watch, too. Whether he had papers or not, I never knew.

Babcock, the third mate, was a slender, blond young fellow, with an open face and quiet manner. He ate after all the rest, silent, thoughtful.

But those were indirect signs. Something else was in the air—over the crew, the passengers, making them watch one another, guard their speech. Everyone seemed to suspect everyone else. The shadow of death, of murder and mystery had descended like a bleak cloud over this mystery cruise.

Trixie slipped into my steward's pantry in the middle of the morning, said: "Well—"

"Well, yourself," I said. "Who did it?"

No wise cracking this morning; we were both serious. "Those two girls are scared to death," Trixie said under her breath. "I saw Miss Lawes slip a little pearl handled automatic under her dress this morning."

I polished a glass slowly, stopped. "We're riding on a

load of dynamite," I said under my breath. "Shields was murdered—and yet there's been no more questions this morning. They act like murder came with the ticket."

Trixie fluffed her hair. She looked like murder wasn't anything.

"Don't let 'em kill you, Mike," she said. "I'd hate to come back without you."

There was a note in her voice I'd heard in my mother's. I waited for the wise crack to follow. It didn't. Trixie was always surprising me.

We came pretty near being friends in that moment as I put a hand on her shoulder. She was only an armful, and suddenly it struck me how I'd miss her if she weren't somewhere around the country, waiting to take my hide off when we met on a job.

Karmos kicked open the door from the gallery. The buzzer snarled on the saloon number and Trixie stepped back, saying sarcastically:

"You wipe glasses like an ashman. Answer your buzzer and I'll polish one like it should be done. How about it, cook?"

Karmos grinned foolishly. Trixie had got to him already—and I liked him less for falling, as I went out and left them alone.

4

MURDER BEHIND,
MYSTERY AHEAD

IT WAS A quiet day, a tense one. Early in the afternoon the course began to change, west for a time, and then heading north, by the sun. I saw a lighthouse off on the horizon. The white, gull-like sails of fishing boats were visible far off, and several times steamers were in sight. I knew these waters roughly. We were swinging around Key West, heading north into the Gulf of Mexico. Through that twenty-odd mile stretch of water between Key West and Marquesas Key.

It knocked into a cocked hat some of my theories. Cuba, the Caribbean, Panama Canal and South America lay south of us. We were heading back up toward the mainland again. Toward seaports, law and order. I still struggled for the answer as the day drew to a close and the Diesel engine still drove us to the north. I went forward during a few spare minutes, to learn what the crew was thinking.

They questioned me. Louie Getta, a sleek, black-haired, olive-skinned young fellow, who had shipped as a sailor, fired question after question.

"How did Shields die?… Who killed him?… What are they saying aft?"

I played stupid, told them what I knew. And the rest of that hard-boiled crew sat around and scowled at me, smoked, raised an occasional question and looked queer. I sensed something under the surface here too, but I couldn't put my finger on it.

I went back to my pantry, wondering. Where was Roger Caldwell and that eight hundred and seventy-five thousand dollars I was supposed to be looking for? Where was his brother? What had the yacht's cruise to do with them? They weren't aboard, that was certain.

And nightfall and dinner went by, and we were still heading into the north. Murder behind us and the tension of death and things about to happen lying thick in the air.

Trixie had nothing to report. The passengers turned in early. I did the same.

Karmos had cleaned up his galley and was already in our little cabin, dealing himself poker hands. He was silent, morose. I noticed that he shuffled the cards and flipped them like an expert. I watched a few hands and saw he was dealing crooked. Karmos was a card sharp. He noticed my scrutiny, boxed the deck and stood up.

"Better turn in," he growled.

"I was thinking so," I agreed.

Karmos pulled a suitcase from under his bunk, opened it and took out a thirty-eight automatic. He pulled the clip and I saw it was full.

"Going gunning for some one?" I asked.

Karmos scowled at me.

"You're too damn curious," he grunted. "Go to sleep and forget everything you see. Get me?"

"Plain enough," I agreed—and began to follow his advice.

Karmos smoked a cigarette, ground the end underfoot, and went out abruptly, saying: "I'm going to get some fresh air."

I would have followed him, but the boat was small. He'd have discovered it. Playing dumb and innocent was my only hope to find out anything. Once I tipped my hand I wouldn't have much chance. But I wondered as I lay in my bunk what Karmos was up to. Was there going to be another killing this night?

I was tired from the night before, fell asleep without knowing it.

And the next thing I knew my habit of hair-trigger sleeping sent me bolt upright in that top berth, listening....

My cabin door had a spring lock, snapping as soon as shut. And I heard as I came awake a faint rasp as the unoiled lock turned.

I slipped the covers back, dropped to the floor in my bare feet and reached the corner behind the door in two steps. Karmos would never be unlocking the door so quietly, so furtively....

The hinges scraped a little as the door opened. I saw the light in the corridor was out. The intruder stepped inside quickly, half shut the door. In the pitch blackness of that tight little cabin I could hear his guarded movements, but I couldn't see him.

How long I had been asleep I didn't know. Karmos might have returned, might be in his bunk. There was no way to tell. No time to think about it. The next moment I dodged, almost gasped aloud.

Four times against the deathly quiet the muffled report of a silenced revolver spat softly.

And I heard four vicious bullets bore into the bedclothes of the lower bunk—Karmos's bunk!

That couldn't be Karmos—or was it? He had taken one gun, might have another one around. It was cold blooded assassination, murder.

And the next moment I went cold, hot, tense with a red flare of rage as two more shots were fired at the pillow of the upper bunk where I had been sleeping.

I would have been slaughtered without ever coming awake. In those pounding seconds, with the acrid smell of smokeless powder in my throat, I realized how risky life on this mysterious yacht had become, how near to death I still was.

A thin pencil of light darted into the upper bunk—and I dove at it.

The man staggered against the berth edge when I struck him, swore aloud, tried to turn on me. I got an arm around his neck, jammed my knees into the back of his legs and jerked back.

He swore again as he went off balance. The back-flailing gun missed my head and smashed into the steel bulkhead against which we both staggered.

I would have had him down but for that bulkhead. I'm a lightweight, but fast. Trouble was nothing new. He topped me by two inches, seemed heavier. But I was behind, forearm locked across his throat. And I had him off balance, gave him no time to get set. We reeled madly in the darkness, met the berths again, careened off to the opposite bulkhead, knocked over a chair there and crashed to the floor.

HE WAS FIGHTING to free himself and get me. But I was fighting with the grim ruthlessness of a doomed man. Those six silenced shots had warned me what to expect. For some reason my number had been turned up. Death had been dealt me, and I won or lost in the next few seconds by my own efforts. I twisted as we fell, came down on top of him. He rolled me off, twisted inside my arm, and tried to brain me with his empty gun.

It just grazed the side of my head, thudding heavily against the floor.

It was too close for comfort. I gambled on my next move. Jerking my arm up under his neck, I jammed the heel of my other palm against his chin. It snapped his head back out of control—snapped it hard, down. The back of his head struck the carpeted floor with another thud.

And I felt the strength run out of him like water as I eeled over on top, set myself and hooked down viciously in the darkness at the spot where his jaw should have been. And I found it with a snapping jar that tingled clear up my arm. He lay still beneath me.

Panting, I staggered up to the light switch. The next moment I was looking down at him. It wasn't Karmos. Jim Lovell, I had heard him give his name in the brief time I had been forward with the crew.

A muscular, square-jawed fellow with a shock of dark hair and an ugly twisted nose that had been broken in some previous fight. He was one of the last men aboard I would have suspected. He had kept quiet, done his work efficiently, and seemingly paid no attention to anyone else. And yet there he was, stirring feebly with returning consciousness. An ugly, silenced, police model thirty-eight revolver on the floor where it had dropped from his fingers. The stench of powder smoke in the air, and the bullets from the gun embedded in our two berths.

Karmos had not returned.

Puzzled, angry, rough, I kicked the door shut and jerked him upright when his eyes opened and his head lifted.

"What's the idea of this, fella?" I bit out.

Lovell shook his head, swiped the back of his hand across a streak of blood at the corner of his mouth. His eyes were wild, harried.

"I don't know," he mumbled—and spat out a broken tooth.

"Says you!"

He saw his gun, moved his hand toward it. I kicked it out of reach, snatched it up, cuffed him on the side of the head. It was no time for kind words.

"Let's have it quick before I brain you!"

Lovell glared at me. He wasn't going to talk. His mouth twitched in a sneer as he eyed me.

Maybe I looked funny in my pajamas. I didn't feel so. And I had met birds like Lovell before.

"Going dumb on me, are you?" I snarled. "Maybe this'll loosen you up!"

And I clouted him over the head with the thin end of the silencer-equipped barrel. When you've just missed assassination by seconds a little rough stuff doesn't matter. And he had handed me a good excuse to break open some of the mystery.

Lovell groaned, clapped his hand to his head groggily.

It came away stained red. He tried to scramble to his feet and I knocked him down again. In my locker drawer was a six-inch knife with a spring blade. I brought it out, snapping the blade open.

"Talk, you yellow rat!" I gave him through my teeth. "Or I'll slit your throat open and swear it was self-defense!"

And it wouldn't have taken much to make me do it. I never did take kindly to being shot in the head while I slept.

Lovell got one look at my face.

"Wait a minute!" he begged thickly.

"Ten seconds, damn you!" I grabbed him by the hair, jerked his head back and waved the knife in front of him. Maybe I looked like a madman, sounded like one. I felt like one.

"My God, *don't!*" Lovell wrenched out. "I'll talk! What do you want to know?"

And just then heavy steps came along the dark passageway. The door was tried. A fist hammered on it. Captain Krupp ordered hoarsely: "Open up here!"

IT HAD ONLY been a few moments since the fight started. The noise must have been heard over half the yacht. I swore under my breath. "Wait a minute."

But that was the break Lovell needed. He yelled before I could stop him, "Captain, he's going to kill me!"

It was all off then. I opened the door. Captain Krupp stepped in, rasping: "What's going on here?" He saw the knife in my hand and Lovell on the floor, the cabin wrecked—and the first question he asked was: "Where's Karmos?"

Queer, wasn't it? Bloody murder before him—and he thought of Karmos.

"Out somewhere," I said. "This rat sneaked in here and pumped bullets in our berths."

Captain Krupp put his brassy stare on me. "You don't seem hurt," he grunted.

Lovell crawled to his feet, eying the knife in my hand. "It was a little joke," he muttered.

"He's the little cut-up, isn't he, Captain?"

Captain Krupp took out a round box of snuff and tucked some under his lip. The veins in his nose were redder than ever. His face was a study.

"So you came back here to play a little joke on your friend, Karmos?" he said in a queer voice.

Lovell nodded. "I knew he was out, so I thought I'd chuck a few bullets in his bedclothes to give him something to think about. Just a little joke, Captain. And when I seen no one in the upper bunk I put a couple there."

"You're a poor liar, Lovell!" I snapped. "You didn't use any light till you'd emptied your gun!" I picked up the small flash he had dropped and put it with his gun.

Captain Krupp reached for them, took them.

"Go forward, Lovell," he ordered. "I'll look into this later."

And I had to stand there while that killer walked out glumly.

Captain Krupp put his brassy stare on me again, sucking at the snuff under his lip. He fingered the flashlight, the gun and silencer. "This is a queer business, steward." He seemed to be thinking hard.

"Very queer, Captain."

"And very suspicious."

"Isn't it?"

"I'll go into this more fully tomorrow," Captain Krupp said heavily. "Go back to sleep. You'll not be bothered again tonight." And he walked out as if a second killing or two might not have been so bad after all.

I smoked a cigarette, boiling mad; and before I finished it a key grated in the lock, and Karmos slipped out of the dark passage and closed the door quietly. His face was red, jaw set, eyes glittering, and he was breathing softly through his teeth as if just emerging from stress of some kind.

"Welcome home, stranger. You just missed a nice assassination."

Karmos looked about the cabin without much interest. "Cigarette," he requested tersely.

I gave him one, and stopped breathing for a moment as I eyed the hand which took it. A smear of fresh red blood discolored the side of his forefinger.

Karmos noticed it, stepped to the washbasin and scrubbed it off. The light glistened back from a large drop of fresh blood on his left shoe. He saw that, too, removed it with his handkerchief.

"Look," I said, "what's the idea of all this? If I'm going to be killed in my sleep I want to know why."

Karmos lighted the cigarette, scowled at me.

"You ask too many questions. If you want to stay healthy, go to sleep and forget about it." Not a word about the blood or what had happened in the cabin. Obviously he wouldn't talk. There seemed to be a conspiracy of silence on every side. Jumpy, nervous, I turned in again, but not to sleep until long after Karmos was snoring. Grim mystery on grim mystery was tangling me badly. Why had Lovell tried to kill Karmos and myself? Why hadn't Captain Krupp done something about it? Whence had come that blood on Karmos's hand and shoe?

What was the outcome of all this going to be?

5

A FLOATING MADHOUSE

IN THE MORNING Lovell was missing.

Some time during the night the engine had slowed. We were slipping along easily through a glassy sea, with the sun on our right and our bow into the northeast. Karmos went to his duties in the galley without a comment on the night's happenings. Captain Krupp, who never seemed to sleep, was shooting sun sights outside the wheelhouse. Anton McSwiggin was standing beside him, looking off the starboard bow through a pair of powerful binoculars.

And when I strained my eyes in that direction I saw the low hazy suggestion of land.

Captain Krupp was not at breakfast. Miss Ward said to me as I set grapefruit in front of her: "There was some excitement last night, steward?"

"Was there, ma'am?"

Anton McSwiggin dug out a spoonful of grapefruit pulp. "You had a nightmare," he said, staring at us. "You heard nothing, did you, steward?" And was there warning in his even monotone?

"I heard nothing," I said.

Miss Ward looked unconvinced, but let the matter drop. I noticed Miss Lawes, the one who had found Shields, watching me covertly all through the meal, but she said nothing.

Babcock, the young mate, seemed nervous, ill at ease. He buttonholed me in the passageway after the meal. "What's this about trouble last night, steward?"

"You heard nothing, sir?"

"I'm a sound sleeper. There was no trouble on my watch before midnight."

He was a nice young fellow, a little vague and confused. I liked him.

"Look here, sir! Do you know anything about all these queer things that are happening?"

His blue eyes looked puzzled, anxious.

"This man Shields was murdered. The captain won't talk about it. And I feel there's something brewing underneath all over the ship, but I can't put my finger on it."

"Neither can I," I confessed. "Lovell slipped into our cabin last night and tried to shoot Karmos and myself with a silenced gun. Our bunks were empty and he missed out."

"Where is he now?"

"The captain sent him forward. I dodged up there before breakfast and he's not around."

Babcock was troubled, hesitant. "I'll talk to you about this later," he said, and went on.

We were heading in toward land. By noon we were passing a low, swampy island, ringed with mangroves, backed by palms, and then other islands as we followed a twisting, winding channel inland.

I knew roughly where we were. Somewhere on the vast, desolate southwestern tip of Florida, one of the most deserted and god-forsaken spots in the whole United

States. Back of the low mangrove jungle on the broken coast line, back of the palms and reeds were the coastal swamps and everglades, a thousand inlets and winding channels. Torpid, sluggish tidal rivers and bayous. Thousands of square miles of swampy jungle and reedy morass, inhabited only by scaly alligators, writhing snakes and great flocks of semi-tropical birds.

An occasional market fisherman or egret plume-poacher was all the human life one would find in this mangrove and salt grass, palmetto and cypress wilderness. And yet the *Stardust* was pushing boldly in on some bit of secret business....

Lunch was a sketchy affair. Krupp and McSwiggin were in the wheelhouse.

Everybody who could get on deck was watching the shore. Even Karmos kept popping his head out the galley door.

I had a word with Babcock in the passage. "Where are we going, sir?"

Babcock shook his head. "Haven't the slightest idea, steward."

THE SHORELINE NARROWED in more and more. The anchor was finally dropped with a harsh rattle of chain. We swung silently, idly, in torpid brownish water.

Captain Krupp bawled orders. The crew lowered one of the two small mahogany motorboats lashed on the upper deck. A rope ladder was dropped over the side.

"Finley, Monohan, get down in the boat!" Captain Krupp ordered.

They were two of the toughest eggs in the crew. Finley was a thin, wiry, bald-headed man with bat-like ears, shifty eyes, and a twisted, sneering mouth. He talked with a Brooklyn accent, swore constantly, carried a chip on his shoulder.

Monohan was a bull chested gorilla with hands like hams and beetling black brows over small cunning eyes. They jumped down in the launch without any apparent curiosity, and Finley went to work on the motor like a man who knew his business.

He had it started inside a minute, and Captain Krupp joined them.

Anton McSwiggin came from his cabin, face expressionless; bony, hooked features looking more like a bird of prey than ever. Without a word to anyone, he climbed over the rail and backed down the ladder.

I was standing close to the rail as McSwiggin stepped into the launch. The bottom of his coat brushed open, revealing a gun belt, loaded with cartridges, around his waist!

They cast off immediately, sheered away from the yacht and knifed through the brown, unhealthy water toward a spot some hundred yards away where the mangroves narrowed in abruptly and a twisting channel snaked from view ahead of them.

And as they went I saw Miss Lawes gripping the rail until the knuckles shone white on the back of her hand. Her face was set, flushed with a hate that was not pretty.

"Get the lunch dishes cleaned up," Karmos said to me— and since it was part of my work I went to the galley. But as I slopped on soapy water my thoughts were on that gunbelt around Anton McSwiggin's waist. What was the answer to that?

Karmos did not come into the galley. It was about ten minutes later when Trixie suddenly entered.

Trixie's little face was tense, excited.

"Mike, there's something wrong!" she said under her breath.

"You don't say!" I marveled. "Maybe we'd better tell teacher!"

Trixie bristled. "This is no time to be smart, Bigmouth. That Lawes girl is acting queer. I just heard a groan in her cabin, and when I knocked she told me to go away and not bother her."

I grinned and wrung out the dishrag. "You've got ears like a bluenose snooper, Brighteyes. She was probably repeating her catechism."

Trixie put her little hands on her little hips and glared at me.

"I know a groan when I hear it, Mike Harris! I tell you there's something wrong! I want you to look into it."

"Sho', sho', baby," I agreed indulgently. "And the more I look the less I see. We're on a floating madhouse, and we'll get our throats cut, or lose our sanity before it's over."

"You never had any sanity!" Trixie said waspishly.

And before I could take up that little question, a sudden outburst of loud talk on the port side brought me out of the galley. The argument was up on the boat deck, and plenty of it. I ran up the nearest companion steps.

Three members of the crew were facing Karmos and Louie Getta. The second motorboat was swung out over the rail. Daly, another hard egg, who topped Karmos by inches, but wasn't as broad, was yelling: "And I say you don't put that boat over the side!"

Karmos swore at him. "It's going over! Captain's orders!"

"That's a goddam lie!" Daly shouted. "He gave no orders like that! And you're staying aboard until he cames back! Come on, men, run 'im away from here!"

Daly stepped forward, bunching his fists.

I saw Louie Getta shrink back against the rail like a coiling snake. His hand slipped under his coat in the old familiar gesture I knew so well. He was packing a gun under there, was ready to use it.

But Karmos stepped in front of him, circling back so that Daly swung over by the rail. Karmos's shirt collar was open. His hand flashed to the back of his neck as he crouched, leaped forward....

And so quick did it happen that the knife which flashed in Karmos's hand was buried in Daly's throat before any of us realized what was happening.

Daly staggered, uttered a grisly, choking scream. His hands made a fluttery lift to his throat....

And then Karmos struck him, drove him against the rail, caught him by the back of his legs and heaved hard. Daly shot back over the rail like a limp bundle. A loud splash floated up.

I jumped to the rail, saw the water roiling over the spot where Daly had vanished, dark, sullen swamp water that hid all it took. A red stain swirled slowly to the surface.

Daly did not come up. And a cold, icy feeling crawled down my back as I thought of him huddled in the oozy mud under the keel of that graceful, white yacht.

Karmos's flat face was twisted in a grinning mask of rage as he crouched, facing the other two.

"Come on, you rats!" he spat at them. "Which of you wants to go next?"

Louie Getta stood rigid, watchful, his hand caught under his coat.

DALY MUST HAVE been egging the other two on. They backed away hastily. "Good God, if you w-want to take the boat that bad, take 'er!" the nearest stammered hastily.

"Get forward where you belong!" Karmos snarled.

The two of them went like whipped dogs. Karmos whirled to me. "Who told you to come up here?"

My gun was down in the cabin. I was still in the dark as to what it was all about. I slid a glance at Louie Getta, whose eyes were burning like black lashed coals. I thought of Daly, of Lovell, of Sam Shields. And remembered I was on board to discover things, not to get carved up fighting blindly.

"Right," I agreed. "If you feel that way about it." And I went down off that boat deck without any more argument.

Louie Getta and Karmos brought that launch down to the water with a rush, cast off the falls, shoved offside and had the motor going in a few moments. And they too steered toward that twisted, snake-like channel, vanishing back in the mangroves.

A stunned silence seemed to fall over the yacht. None of the girls was in evidence. The two men who had fled the boat deck were huddled in the bow, muttering together.

Trixie reached me at the rail. White faced, determined. "They murdered a man!" she gulped.

"Just put a knife in his throat."

"What's going to happen?" Trixie whispered.

"At the rate they're killing them off the yacht will be

empty in about five more days." I looked at the second launch just vanishing among the mangroves. "Where's Babcock?" I asked Trixie abruptly.

"Why—why, I haven't seen him."

"Queer he didn't show up while they were shouting on the upper deck."

"Have they killed him?" Trixie gulped.

"Probably," I said grimly.

And right there I realized it was time for Mike Harris to chuck the role of steward and deal himself a hand. Wholesale murder was pushing things a little too far.

"Where's this Lawes girl?" I snapped.

"In her cabin, I guess."

"Come on! Get her to open the door. I want to talk to her."

Trixie knocked.

The Lawes girl snapped: "Who is it?"

"Stewardess, ma'am."

"Go 'way! I don't want to see you!"

"It's something important, ma'am," little Trixie says meekly.

A moment's silence, and then: "All right. I'll be out."

The spring lock was turned. She opened the door a few inches, slipped out, slamming it behind her. And startled surprise flashed across her face when she saw me. The next instant it was hard. "What do you want?" she asked in a brittle voice.

"Save it," I said calmly. "What are you hiding in your cabin for?"

"I wasn't! What I do is none of your business! Go away!"

"There's been another man killed," I said. "Karmos, the cook, knifed one of the crew."

"Is that so?" she asked indifferently. No surprise, regret, dismay, apprehension.

"I'll have a look in your cabin," I decided.

She turned feline, dangerous, as her hand fumbled with a small beaded bag she had brought out with her. It was opened before my eyes dropped from her face.

A little pearl handled revolver was covering me.

"Get back! Get away!" she hissed. "There'll be another dead man if you butt into something that's none of your business!"

And she meant it, the hellcat! I flashed a look at Trixie. We were on familiar ground now. "Watch that thing, it'll go off," I warned sharply.

And Trixie's hand slipped forward, knocking the gun to one side. Its explosion sounded thunderous in that narrow passage as she did her best to get me. I twisted the gun out of her hand a moment later.

"Off the stage for you, lady!" I growled. "Open that door! Don't make me strip you down to find the key!"

She was pale, panting. One look at my face and the key came out of the purse. I opened the door, swore under my breath.

Babcock, the young mate, was lying on her single berth, ankles tied, wrists handcuffed behind him, mouth gagged.

I had him on his feet in short seconds. "It must be leap year," I said. "Wouldn't you marry the gal?"

Babcock rubbed his wrists. His face was flushed, angry.

"Karmos, the cook, did this! The girl asked me to come to her cabin quick. Karmos was waiting inside. I didn't have

much chance to get at her gun. She's been watching me to
see that I keep quiet."

"Why?" I asked the dame.

She stood, tall, stately, silent. She shrugged stubbornly.

"Okay," I said. "Go dumb and like it, sister. Flop down
on the berth there."

SHE GAVE ME a good roundhouse oath and said she'd be
damned if she would.

"Tut-tut, such naughty language!" I said sadly, and
picked her up and slammed her down on the berth in
spite of her scrapping.

"You'll be sorry for this!" she panted, glaring at me.

"I'm sorry already," I confessed, hauling one of her wrists
under the berth rail. I handcuffed her wrists around that
stout steel rail, saying: "If you were a lady I'd be still sorrier.
Now lie there and squall if you want to. It'll take this key
or a hacksaw to get you loose. And if you're not good I may
swallow the key."

I locked her in. "Get your gun," I said to Trixie.

"I've got it already," Trixie said, patting the front of her
dress.

"Lock yourself in your cabin then."

"No!" Trixie said stubbornly.

"All right, come along." And as I led the way to my cabin
I hurriedly sketched to Babcock what had happened.

"Good God!" he groaned. "This is terrible! They're all
madmen!"

"I don't die any more willingly for a madman," I said
grimly.

We were in my cabin by then. I jerked out a suitcase,

stuffed my automatic, an extra clip and two boxes of cartridges in my pocket.

"Got a gun?" I said to Babcock.

"Yes. Always have one in my luggage in case of mutiny."

"This is mutiny and mayhem. Get your gun."

And as I followed him out of the door I pushed Trixie back and locked her in. "I'll know you're safe in there," I called through the door.

Trixie was wild. But she only hurt her foot when she kicked the door. "I'll settle with you for this, Mike Harris!" she promised furiously.

"Be a lady, if you can remember the rules," I advised cheerfully, and followed Babcock, feeling easier in my mind about Trixie.

"There's a dinghy left on the upper deck with an outboard motor stowed in it," I said to him. "We're going to take that and look into this."

Babcock was a young fellow. It was probably his first serious trouble. "Maybe we'd better stay here," he said excitedly.

"Nix. I've got a hunch. We may be too late yet." And I told him who I was and what I was after.

"I see," said Babcock. He quieted, grew thoughtful, ran his fingers through his blond hair. "Maybe you're right. Let's go."

No one stopped us; we got that dinghy over the side. I shipped the outboard motor over the stern, made sure the tank was full of gas, got it started, and we *put-putted* furiously away after the other two boats.

My last look back showed the yacht floating on the brown, glassy water as innocently and gracefully as a harm-

less white swan. But my mind was on that limp, ooze-cra-
dled body beneath it.

We were suddenly driving up a narrow, twisting channel
where fish flashed in shoals through the dark water, and the
dank mangrove roots rose like snaky arms from the muddy
banks. Kingfishers flashed into sight and out. A great blue
heron rose off stilt-like legs and flapped heavily away.

The brassy sun, dropping in the western sky, poured heat
against the back of our necks. A snake slid off a mangrove
root and vanished in the water. And as we rounded a turn
suddenly the torpedo-like rush of a big alligator smashed
into the water. Babcock peered about, looked uneasy.

I didn't blame him. Murder behind—and swampy
wilderness ahead. Palmetto and saw grass, cypress and
mangrove, low tangles of bushes on the higher ground, and
now and then a gaunt dead tree lifting weathered studs to
the brassy sky. And where were we going? What were we
looking for? What would we find?

It was sheer luck that channel did not break into a dozen
tortuous courses as so many channels along this coast did.
But it narrowed as it wound inland. Our luck couldn't hold.

It didn't. The channel suddenly ran into an island, split
into three channels, and we were lost. I cut the motor.

Babcock looked around at me, troubled. "Sure we're
right? Not a sign of those boats."

"They came this way."

And like a signal, impacting with startling sharpness on
the desolate quiet, came a gunshot off to the left.

We took that left channel, narrower yet, tortuous,
ominous. And the land to each side rose higher, drier.
The mangroves thinned. Palmetto, sawgrass, grew thicker.

Twice I stopped the motor, heard no more shots. And we rounded a short, abrupt turn, Saw a dirty towel tied to a long stick planted in the bank. Saw three boats moored to a rickety board landing; two of them the launches from the yacht, the other a lumbering fisherman's boat with a low deckhouse forward. Motor dead, we coasted in to the bank.

"Good God!" Babcock said in a strangled voice. "Look at that!"

Half in, half out the water, face down in the muddy grass, bald, naked head white and grisly in the sun, lay Finley.

6

DEATH IN THE SWAMP

FINLEY WAS DEAD, killed by a terrific blow back of one ear. I saw the wrench that did it as I beached the dinghy and leaped ashore.

The rotting odor of decay, the stillness of death lay heavy, ominous over the spot. Then a bird warbled merrily, mockingly. The dull green leaves of the nearby mangroves stirred restlessly in a slight breeze. Our guns were in our hands now.

Babcock said in a hushed, strained voice: "Are they insane, killing this way?"

"Some call it that," I said drily. "You know what you're up against now. Don't go on unless you're willing to face it out."

Babcock was no coward. His jaw shoved out stubbornly; he rapped quickly: "Don't worry."

We had spoken under our breaths. Now I led the way into a narrow winding path which struck back from the water. The trampled saw grass showed that it had been used much recently, after a long interval when no foot had trod this way.

For a quarter of a mile that path wound back through a tangle of palmetto, shoulder high reeds and grass, lush bushes, trees and vines. It was semitropical wilderness, seldom disturbed by man. And I walked with my trigger finger set. There was no law but that of might and craftiness on this desolate coast.

Suddenly I stopped so abruptly that Babcock bumped into my back. A small clearing lay before me. Backed up against the brush at my right was a small, sprawling palmetto shack. It had no windows. A sun canopy of palmetto leaves sagged drunkenly from posts set before it. But that was not what made me crouch, throw out a hand in warning, stifle the exclamation that almost left my lips.

Monohan, the big bull chested sailor, lay less than thirty feet away at the front corner of the palmetto shack. Lay on his back, arms outflung, sightless eyes staring at the blue bowl of the sky. The flies were already thick over the blood staining the front of Monohan's shirt.

Babcock sucked breath sharply through his teeth. I flashed a glance over my shoulder, saw him staring rigidly at the sight. I beckoned him down behind the low screening bushes at my right shoulder, for the sharp murmur of a voice drifted through the windowless walls of that clumsy shack. In there was the answer to this carnival of death.

The shack faced the way we were looking, its side to us, its back against the tangle of brush through which we had come. There were chinks in the palmetto walls through which a man in the open could be seen. I had to risk it.

"Stay here," I whispered to Babcock, and, crouching, walked softly through the trampled grass to the end of the shack. And when I crouched at the rear corner and put my ear close I knew why I had not been observed. No one inside was thinking of the outside. I heard Karmos speaking in a dull, vicious tone.

"I'm through talkin'! I'll give you thirty seconds more before I plug you both between the eyes, an' start lookin' myself."

A hoarse, labored, unrecognizable voice replied: "You won't find it."

"I'll save one for you," Karmos promised. "And before I'm through he'll pray for a chance to talk. Come on—thirty seconds!"

"I'll be damned if I talk!" the hoarse voice burst out frantically.

And I knew that when those short seconds passed another man would never see the setting sun.

The sobsisters would say I rose to the brave call of duty. I didn't. But red anger at this cold disregard of life forced my hand. I looked at Babcock, crouching there at the end of the path, beckoned him on, and slipped to the front, where the flies made sport with Monohan.

And as I went, Karmos bit out: "Fifteen seconds!"

A blanket which had covered the doorway lay trampled on the hard packed ground before the door.

"Five seconds, damn you!" Karmos warned harshly—and I jumped through the door and yelled:

"Put 'em up!"

It was complete surprise—for all of us. I looked for four men and found six.

Louie Getta, standing to the left of the door, gun in hand, whirled to shoot. I shot the gun out of his hand. Swearing in a ready, pain-lashed falsetto, he staggered back, clutching his mangled fingers.

Karmos, back to me, gun in one hand, eyes on the watch in his other hand, jumped, whirled, dropped his gun and shoved his hands up when he saw my automatic swing on him.

"Don't shoot!" he yelled.

"Maybe I will yet," I said. "Get over there with Getta!"

He did, hastily. And when Babcock burst through the door I grabbed Karmos's gun.

"Good God—what's coming off in here?" Babcock burst out, jaw dropping.

Anton McSwiggin and Captain Krupp were standing against the back wall of the shack. The shack was bare inside with the exception of a couple of packing cases, a litter of luggage and an army cot against the wall at each end. In the middle of the floor, spread-eagled to stakes driven in the dirt, lay two men. Their faces were bruised, bloody, their eyes wild, despairing, and their wrists chafed raw where they had struggled against the cords holding them. I have never seen such wild joy as flashed on those two faces at sight of Babcock and myself.

ANTON MCSWIGGIN'S BONY, angular face looked relieved too as he stepped forward. "You men got here just in time," he said. "Babcock, take those two men down to the launches and hold them for mutiny and murder."

"Did they kill Monohan?" Babcock gulped.

"Yes," Anton McSwiggin said sorrowfully. "Shot him down in cold blood. They'll have to be ironed."

Karmos laughed harshly. "So that's it—"

He said no more, for Captain Krupp sprang forward with cat-like quickness and smashed him full in the mouth.

"That'll be enough out of you!" Krupp snarled. "I'm running this party again!"

A red trickle of blood seeped out of the corner of Karmos's mouth. He stood still, silent, with a queer grin on his face. I couldn't understand that grin.

"Who are you?" the nearest man on the floor asked me hoarsely.

I recognized the voice—the one I had heard defying Karmos. His eyes searched my face. He was a man in his middle forties, thin, sallow, unshaven now. Some of the wild joy and relief had vanished from his face.

"Who am I?" I said. "Why, I'm the steward on McSwiggin's yacht. And my friend here is the mate."

The second man, several years younger, thin too, but hard, defiant, laughed harshly. "Out of the frying pan into the fire," he grated.

"Shut up!" Krupp barked at him.

Anton McSwiggin's pale stare wandered over Babcock and myself. "A good job, men," he said. "You will be suitably rewarded."

"I'll bet we will," I grunted. "I suppose you know your man Finley has been killed too?"

"Is that so?" he said without much surprise.

"It not only is so, it's a fact, Mr. McSwiggin. And there's a hell of a lot of explaining going to be done right here."

"I shall be glad to explain anything," McSwiggin assented smoothly, "What is it you want to know, steward?"

"You'd be surprised," I snapped. "First, who are these two men? Who pegged them out on the floor this way?"

Captain Krupp had been busy in the corner with Karmos and Louie Getta. Babcock was standing next to me, still a little foggy, but willing. Krupp stepped over behind us, and while I waited for McSwiggin to answer, the barrel of a gun was jammed in my back so hard I almost yelled with pain. Out of the corner of my eye I saw Babcock jump, utter a startled exclamation.

Captain Krupp yelled in our ears: "Drop those guns, both of you!"

He had us. And something in the tone of his voice told me that he meant what he said. Babcock's gun hit the floor. Mine followed.

"Get 'em, McSwiggin!"

Anton McSwiggin stepped over one of the prostrate men and picked up our guns. His big knobby, red hands handled them with familiar ease.

McSwiggin sneered under his big hooked nose. He looked like a triumphant bird of prey. He spoke softly, malevolently.

"So you want to know who pegged those men, steward? I did, and I owe you many thanks for blundering in here and surprising Karmos."

McSwiggin did not raise his voice as his pale eyes wandered to the corner where Karmos and Louie Getta stood.

"Everything is all right now, isn't it, Karmos?"

I turned my head and saw Karmos shudder. Yes, he shuddered, that stocky, hard-boiled Greek, and I didn't blame him much. Things unspeakable crawled in McSwiggin's soft voice.

Krupp chuckled loudly, prodded me roughly with the gun.

"I've had you down for a nosy bug ever since you came

aboard, steward. And now you're going to learn a lot," He laughed again.

Babcock said angrily, "I say, Captain, this is no way to be treating me."

"Sure it ain't," Captain Krupp agreed jovially. "But wait a little—and you'll think this is pretty nice."

Louie Getta had wrapped a handkerchief around his bloody hand. He spoke to me spitefully. "You fool, we would have let you go! Now those two will kill you like a rat! You know too much. You should have had sense enough to know what was coming when Sam Shields was killed."

"So they killed Shields?" I says softly.

McSwiggin showed his teeth at me. "Lovell did," he corrected. "And Karmos, I'm not forgetting you killed Lovell. I can't prove it—but I know."

Karmos shrugged.

"Did you want me to wait for him to knock me off in my bunk?"

"It might have been better for you," McSwiggin smiled. "And now," he said gently, "we'll see if Mr. Caldwell can't be persuaded to tell where he's hidden all that money."

"So this is Roger Caldwell?" I said, although I had been pretty sure of it all along.

Caldwell rolled his head at me, nodded weakly. "Yes," he said with an effort. "And this Anton McSwiggin I trusted has double-crossed me. He is a fiend!"

It was melodrama, but I didn't feel like smiling. Caldwell seemed to have put the thing neatly.

McSwiggin enjoyed it.

"Eight hundred thousand dollars is a lot of money, Caldwell. You should have known that my acquaintance with your brother was not quite enough. And anyway your idea of having a safe, joyful cruise around the world wouldn't have worked. Sam Shields knew it wouldn't. He and his wife took Karmos and Getta in with them, and were waiting to snatch that money. Just because Shields fenced a few of your securities and handed me the money to buy the yacht was no proof he could be trusted.

"He'd have done the same as Karmos here just tried to do—got the money, killed you, escaped up the coast and lived soft for a while."

AND SUDDENLY THE whole thing pieced together clearly in my mind. Caldwell had known he had to get out of the country. Through his brother he had contacted the underworld, Shields and Anton McSwiggin. Shields had cashed some of the securities; Anton McSwiggin had bought the yacht; and Caldwell and his brother had lain low in this inaccessible spot on the south Florida coast, waiting for the yacht to come around, pick them up and head for distant ports.

The thing was involved, but clear. McSwiggin had played for the whole eight hundred thousand instead of a small split. Krupp was his man, Lovell had been his man, Finley and Monohan also.

Shields had been thinking the same thing. His wife, who passed as Miss Lawes, Karmos and Getta, there in the corner, had been biding their time.

Krupp and McSwiggin had removed Shields, tried to get Karmos, and they had left the yacht for this meeting with Roger Caldwell and his brother, intending to settle Karmos when they got back.

And Karmos and Getta had put Babcock out of the way temporarily and hastened after to be in at the death. Money mad, all of them. Reckless of life and safety, before the chance to get their hands on almost a million dollars in cash.

What a fool Caldwell had been to think he could put it over this way.

Anton McSwiggin's eyes slid to me. "How did you know who this man was, steward?"

"I read the papers."

He believed me, ignored me, looking down at Roger Caldwell.

"I saw a big ant hill out there in the sun," he murmured. "I know a better way than shooting, Caldwell. We'll just move these stakes out there and peg you over that ant hill. You've read of that, haven't you? In less than an hour you'll talk."

I didn't blame Roger Caldwell for shuddering, for graying, for beginning to tremble. An hour of sun and ants would reduce the strongest man to a gibbering idiot. A short while longer would bring death, horrible, certain. Caldwell broke, talked.

"You'd do it, damn you!" he wrenched out. "The stuff's in a waterproof box, buried on the south side of that big tree, a hundred and seven paces from the south corner of the building."

Anton McSwiggin exhaled a soft breath of relief. A wolfish, feverish blaze leaped in his eyes. This was the end of the trail for him—eight hundred thousand dollars, and not a squawk would be made about it. Caldwell couldn't afford to talk—if he lived.

Krupp was standing behind Babcock and myself when Karmos hurled his squat, powerful body through the thin palmetto wall of that shack. I guess he figured it was the only chance he had.

The gun came out of my back. Krupp whirled with an oath on his lips. McSwiggin did too. Both of them shot fast and quick.

It was the break I had been waiting for. And I took it. For I knew Babcock and I weren't going back to the yacht to talk. Men with eight hundred grand to spend don't want a murder charge against them. They'd figure some way to explain our disappearance.

I spun on my toes, hooking a fist from my waist. I was light. Krupp was heavy, with a ponderous jaw. But I smashed my fist under his jaw, square into his throat.

Delivered right, there is no deadlier blow. Krupp gagged, went vacant, limp, collapsed. And I tore the nearest gun from his nerveless fingers as he went down, retching, half unconscious. I was swinging back to Anton McSwiggin before he saw what was happening, swinging, dodging at the same time. He shot, and he was a good shot. It caught me in the shoulder even as I dodged, ripping through the upper muscle. But years of target practice paid out in moments like this. I shot the gun out of his hand an instant later.

But he had two guns, might have got me with the second. Dazed, startled, Babcock abruptly came to life. Out of the corner of my eye I saw him leave the floor and dive at McSwiggin. His shoulder struck McSwiggin's knees. The second gun crashed futilely as he slammed McSwiggin to the floor. I couldn't shoot then. I whirled to look for Louie

Getta as Babcock and McSwiggin rolled over those two helpless captives pegged out on the floor.

KARMOS LAY IN a crumpled heap outside the splintered hole he had torn in the frail end-wall. And Louie Getta had seized the split seconds of opportunity and plunged out that hole also. He was gone, unarmed, wounded, panicky—a good riddance.

Babcock could fight like a wild man when he had to. When I looked next he had McSwiggin's gun hand pinned to the floor and was throttling him with the other hand.

I had the gun a moment later. We had McSwiggin and no opposition.

Panting, we grinned at each other through the drifting veils of powder smoke.

"Good boy!" I says. "There's a camp shovel over there in the corner. Take a gun and run get that box. Keep your eye peeled for Louie Getta. He still might feel reckless."

"I'll be looking for him," Babcock promised with set jaw.

And while Babcock hurried off I kicked the groaning McSwiggin down flat on his face, and sat on him.

"You've made a mistake, steward!" he jerked out. "How would four hundred thousand dollars look to you?"

"Great!" says I, and kicked him again just for luck. I couldn't forget all those dead men, whether they brought it on themselves or not.

"I'll give you four hundred thousand cash if you'll let me have that box and get away with it," he promised.

"Piker!" says I. "I've got a better idea. I'll take it all and return it to the office it was stolen from."

Roger Caldwell hadn't learned a thing. He still had larceny in his soul. "I'll give you half a million," he promised feverishly. "You won't get a hundredth of that if you play the fool and return it."

"Thanks for nothing," I told him. "It'll be reward enough when I see the lot of you in the pen. I've dealt with crooks for a long time, but you rats take the cake."

"You're mighty honest for a steward," McSwiggin sneered with his face in the dirt.

"I'm mighty honest for anybody," I said cheerfully. "The name is Harris. The boss is the Blaine Detective Agency. And the answer is plenty of law for all of you. Suckers!"

Roger Caldwell, groaned, shut up, and the fight went out of McSwiggin. Babcock brought a big tin box back. We checked through thick sheaves of high denomination currency, wads of easily peddled securities. Most of it was there.

Karmos was dead. Monohan was dead. Louie Getta got away with one of the boats. We could afford to lose him.

Babcock and I trussed up the Caldwell half-brothers, Krupp and McSwiggin, marched them down to the fast launch Getta left and took them back to the yacht.

We had the guns, the authority and the evidence to get that yacht back to Key West without any trouble.

And we did.

The two dames who had been tipped off they would soon see their friends, the Caldwells, took it hard. But my most exciting moment was when I let Trixie Meehan out. What a girl! What a tongue! What a vocabulary!

And then she saw my wounded shoulder and broke down. We had kind words.

"You're an awful fool, Ape!" says Trixie later as she dressed my shoulder. "Suppose you had been killed?"

"Now that you mention it, you frighten me," I grinned. "But I'm tough. I can even put up with you."

And then as usual we ended the case with unkind words.

FALLING DEATH

*The Dead Pilot and the Burning Plane That
Came Tumbling Out of the Sky Were Samples
of the Horror That Mike Harris Had to Face*

1

A TOUGH ASSIGNMENT

THE MESSAGE CAUGHT me in church at high noon playing best man to Ramsey Rogers. That was an ordeal. When the dominie asked if there was any reason why this man and this woman should not be united in holy matrimony and looked expectantly over the gathering, I held my breath. Ramsey grew a little pale himself.

But Ramsey was still a lap ahead of his sins and a few minutes later was married for better or worse to the little blonde who had snatched him out of circulation.

I took my toll from the bride, noted that her bouquet was caught by a divorcee who had been over the route three times, and was getting set to head for the wedding breakfast when an elderly usher who was a relative of the bride pushed through to me.

"Mr. Michael Harris," he gave me with a lather of dignity.

"Mike Harris to you today, friend."

"A message has been delivered at the church door for you, Mr. Harris. I gathered that the matter is urgent."

"Too late," I wisecracked. "Good old Ramsey is landed and I can't stop it for the gal. She should have subpoenaed him."

*His gun swung toward the
corner where I was standing*

And then the snooty usher jumped as I read the message and swore.

> *Get over to the office as quick as you can. I need you.*
> *Thompson.*

I had been half expecting something like that. My week's vacation was two day old, and they never went more than three without something breaking. How Thompson had found me was a mystery. I thought I had covered my tracks for the whole week. But then that was in his line. Thompson was the eastern manager for the Blaine Detective Agency, and the office was the international headquarters

*As the man fell forward on
his face, a frightened voice
inside yelled: "The cops!"*

for the great Blaine organization, taking up two floors on
Forty-sixth Street off the avenue.

Thompson had me hooked. There was no "out" when he
sent a call like that. I washed my hands of society and the
wedding party and became plain Mike Harris, detective,
once more. A taxi rushed me down to Forty-sixth Street.
An elevator shot me up to the eighteenth floor. And I blew
into Thompson's office expecting the worst.

I got it.

Thompson leaned back in his chair and ran his eye over
the morning coat and striped trousers, the wing collar and
patent leather shoes. He pulled the frayed stump of a cigar
out of his mouth and snorted.

"I beg pawdon, my good man," he said in a Piccadilly

accent he had picked up in the London office. "Did I break
in on your bally social schedule? Deucedly sorry."

"It's a gag," I says. "It's been so long since a gentleman
has been seen around these offices I thought I'd hand one
around for inspection."

"You shouldn't have come along then," Thompson
suggested, and got down to business. "Know anything
about airplanes, Mike?"

"They go up and they come down," I said brightly. "I
used to fly kites."

"Sap!" Thompson grinned, jamming his cigar back in
one corner of his mouth and rolling it over to the other.

"Didn't I see a flying license once with your name on it,
and half a thousand hours checked off? You were a tramp
flyer for a time back there after the war, weren't you?"

"You did and I was," I admitted. "I barnstormed in crates
that would give some of these modern ice cream flyers the
heaving jitters."

"They were men in those days, eh?" Thompson said
sarcastically. "Well, here's your chance to be a man again.
What do you think of this chap?"

Thompson reached back on his desk, pulled out a snap-
shot and handed it to me. It was a thin, horse-faced young
man wearing Oxford bags and a polo coat, with a monocle
screwed in one eye and a vacant expression surrounding
a big nose.

"I rate him subnormal, with a twisted IQ and an average of about thirty-six," I told Thompson. "And on second
thought after looking at that monocle some more I'll knock
off the averages all around. He looks like he was dropped as
a child and never got over it. Who is he and why?"

"HE IS YOU and you are him," Thompson said, reaching for the picture. "I've fixed it up by cable. That young man is one of our brightest Continental operators, and he's laid up right now with a broken leg. You take over his identity in the States for the time being. You are the Honorable Cecil Wormley-Squires, of Wormley Hall, Sussex, ex-officer of His Majesty's Royal Flying Corps, ex-civilian pilot, here on a good will mission to visit your old friend Wilbur Gleason of Gleason, Incorporated. Do I make myself plain?"

"With a bang," I said. "You're indisposed. You ate too much. It's the heat. I never was a Wormley-Squires—and what's more, I become one over my dead body, Sussex or no Sussex! This Gleason, Incorporated, is the airplane factory, isn't it?"

"Correct," Thompson nodded, smiling like the cat that swiped the cream. "Know him?"

"No," says I, "but I know all about him. He's pre-war vintage. Back in the days of the old box kite models he built 'em and flew 'em, and he's been doing it ever since. The Gleason transport is one of the sweetest we've got today."

"I see you read the papers at least," Thompson commented brightly. "The Gleason people subscribe to our protection service."

"Do they?" I yawned.

That wasn't anything unusual. Thousands of stores, offices, banks and factories did the same thing. Our greatest trouble with them was small change larceny. The local offices usually handled it.

Thompson rolled his cigar to the other side of his mouth, crossed an ankle over a knee, and flicked a bit of lint off his leg.

"The Gleason people have lost a piece of paper," he said laconically.

"They've lost what?"

"A piece of paper."

"Now just think of that," says I sarcastically. "A piece of paper. My, my! What was it? A ten thousand dollar bill or the deed to the factory?"

"No," said Thompson, and bit down hard on the end of his cigar. His eyes went cold, I knew that look, and leaned forward, all attention. "No," said Thompson, "I wish it were a gag. Unfortunately a man was murdered before that paper was stolen. The watchman at the factory, to be exact. Gleason had locked the paper in his desk drawer. When the watchman failed to telephone the police at midnight an investigation was made at once. He was found dead in the hall outside Gleason's office. Nothing seemed to be disturbed. The safe hadn't been touched. Gleason was called at once, of course, and at first reported everything all right. But this morning when he opened his desk drawer to get that paper, it was missing. He got in touch with us at once."

"Why all this fuss over a sheet of paper?" I asked curiously.

Thompson shrugged.

"Gleason will explain. There seems to be an extraordinary and very serious situation there. The plant is in Chicago, you know. Our Chicago office called me first, making a report of the matter and suggesting we assign someone to help out. Then Gleason came in on the wire a little later, yelping for assistance. He seems to be badly stirred up. I thought of Squires and suggested that I send a man as him, to visit Gleason. He said it was just the thing. I suggest you get an outfit together and catch the first train. How soon can you leave?"

"This afternoon," I said, glancing at my wrist watch. "Give me that snap and some expense money."

"Good," said Thompson. "Wire Gleason from the train that you're coming, and sign it Squires. Anything else?"

"No," I sighed. "But if I come out of this talking with an English accent, I'll haunt you."

2

FACTS OF DEATH

MIKE HARRIS LEFT the taxi at Fifth Avenue and Forty-second Street. And two hours later the Honorable Cecil Wormley-Squires came up at Fifty-eighth Street with everything complete, including a briar pipe and a humidor of the Prince's own mixture. I had steamship plasters on my bags, London labels in my clothes and English bank notes and shillings in my pocket.

The steamship arrivals in the afternoon papers told me that the *Gastonia* had docked that morning. So I taxied to the Grand Central, bought a compartment on the next Chicago train, and wired Wilbur Gleason that I had arrived on the *Gastonia,* and would be in Chicago in the morning—"Cheerio—Squires."

That evening I practiced my accent on the porter and dining car waiters, and a couple of business men I met in the club car. By morning I was wondering why the blooming Yanks didn't wipe out the debts like sensible people and assuring the porter that in England we had trains that were trains—"take the Royal Scot, for instance. Longest non-stop train in the world, my good man."

"Yas, suh," said the porter doubtfully. "I s'pect so, suh.

But that's no place fo' me. I heahs dey don' have colo'd po'tahs theah, suh."

"Quite so," I gave him—and we made Chicago.

Wilbur Gleason met me at the train. He was a tall, thin, businesslike man just past his forties. His face was tanned almost black. He moved like an athlete, and his handshake came down on my fingers like a vise.

"Er—Mr. Squires, eh?" he said doubtfully.

"Cecil to you, Wilbur," I said. "And it's ripping to see you again, old chap. Let's see, it's—uh—several years since you were in England, isn't it?"

"Eleven months," he said dryly. "I made a swing through England last summer, visiting the airplane plants. Brush up your memory, Cecil, my friend. I spent a week-end at your place in Sussex, if you remember."

"A Wormley-Squires never forgets," I assured him cheerfully. "We enjoyed your visit no end. And remember when we ran down to Croydon and had a look at those new interceptors the Royal Flying Corps had developed? Plenty of thousand feet a minute climb. You chaps over here will have a beastly time doing better than that. Although I understand your new Curtiss bomber is something a little bit out of the ordinary."

Gleason's face cleared up a little at that. He grinned as he said: "I see you know a little about planes, at that."

"Nine hundred and sixty-three hours on my ticket when I stopped flying about eleven years ago," I admitted.

"I barnstormed in the old Jennys, and anything else that came along. And I've kept up with it since then from an armchair."

"Great!" said Gleason enthusiastically. "We're in luck.

You're just the man for the job!" And he sounded as if he really meant it. Although for a moment he looked a bit doubtful as he glanced down at me.

I knew what he was thinking. I wasn't so big and I wasn't so wide, and sometimes people got the wrong idea. I never could figure why a lot of folks thought it took big men to do things. Take a weasel for instance....

By that time we had led our redcaps outside the station to a green roadster. They stowed the luggage in the back. I tipped them. Gleason took the wheel and tooled the car away from the station.

"Seen the fair yet?" he asked, and when I told him I'd been busy down in Florida parts for some time he drove over that way, talking as we went.

"It's a devil of a mess—er—Squires. By the way, what *is* your real name?"

"The less you know, the less you'll speak out of turn," I grinned. "As you were saying?"

"I was going to say that we're up in the air," Gleason continued. "At least I am. I suppose you know that a sheet of paper has been stolen and a watchman killed."

"I was told that—and not much more," I nodded. "What's the serious situation? How does it happen the local police and our Chicago office can't handle it?"

"This is the Field Museum," Gleason pointed out. "The fair buildings are down to the right. Impressive layout, isn't it?"

"Very," I agreed, and spared them a short look. "I always put business ahead of pleasure, Mr. Gleason. Do you mind?"

"Certainly not. Glad to hear it." Gleason swung the

heavy machine about and we headed back toward Michigan Boulevard.

HE ACTED LIKE a man who had something on his mind, and was trying to cover up while he got his thoughts in order. I saw him studying me out of the corner of his eye.

"Our factory is out at Winstead, on the north shore," he said abruptly. "It's a small suburban town, but it gives us our test field at the door of the factory, and the lake behind us for water landings. In summer Winstead is more or less a summer resort. A great many people from the city have cottages along the shore front. The police force is small and not too efficient, I'm afraid."

Gleason smiled wryly as he said that.

"When it comes to getting at the murder of our night watchman, about the most they can do is suggest someone was after the contents of the office safe, and gave it up when old Tom Sullivan had been killed. A fine old chap, Tom. With me eighteen years, from the old days when I started making planes in an abandoned canning factory."

"Sad," I agreed delicately. "How was he killed? Shot?"

And Gleason's answer floored me. "Knifed in the back," he said harshly. "He didn't have a chance."

"In the hall before your office?"

"Yes."

"Hmm," says I. "Funny. Safe crackers don't run to knives as a rule. Your watchman had to be looking the other way when a knife was planted in his back. In a factory, at night, every little sound is audible. A man with normal ears would hear anyone coming up behind and turn around before he got close enough to use steel. Was there a door the man could have stepped out of?"

Gleason gave me another queer look, full-faced this time.

"No door. What's your idea about it?" he asked me bluntly.

And I had a pat answer for him. "Your watchman must have known the fellow who handled the knife. Known him well enough to let him come close. Known him well enough to feel certain there was no danger in turning his back."

And Gleason nodded slowly as he swung north into the busy traffic lanes of the boulevard.

"That is exactly what occurred to me," he confessed. "Tom carried a loaded revolver. He was an ex-soldier and knew how to use it. He was in his late fifties, but strong and active. If he had caught a stranger there in the hall in the middle of the night, he would never have given the fellow a chance to get behind him." Gleason's voice rose above the sound of the traffic—sharp, bitter.

"The man who was in that hall in the middle of the night, the man who killed Tom Sullivan with a knife so it would make no noise, the man who jimmied open my desk drawer and took that sheet of paper, was a man well known to all of us! He was a man who might have had legitimate business in the factory at night. He probably greeted Tom pleasantly when Tom discovered him there in the hall. And he waited until the old fellow's back was turned and killed him in cold blood!"

"Pleasant people you have in Winstead," I murmured.

Gleason gave me a look almost haggard.

"That's why I turned to the Blaine Agency. I wanted a man of experience. A man who could come in as a stranger and move about without being suspected. For the man who killed Tom Sullivan is still among us. We're working with him, talking to him, meeting him face to face. And I'm afraid that someone else may be murdered before this thing is over. We've got to hunt him down as unobtrusively as possible. Tom was the second one..." Gleason's voice trailed off into silence. He shook his head forebodingly.

"Wait a minute!" I broke out as we rolled past the stone lions in front of the art museum. "What's this about your watchman being the second one?"

"One of our test pilots, Art Ahern, was killed three weeks ago while testing a new plane," Gleason said. "He came down in a spin from a few hundred feet and crashed before he could bail out of the cockpit and use his chute. The plane burned with him. But in the wreckage we found a control wire that had been filed almost in two.

"It was a deliberate case of sabotage, with murderous intent!"

"Bad!" said I—and really meant it.

In my mind's eye I was seeing that poor devil going into the spin, fighting the controls, wondering wildly what had happened to them. It was a nasty picture, one that has probably occurred to every man who has taken a plane into the air.

Gleason nodded soberly.

"A FEW MINUTES before Ahern went up on that flight he came to my office in some agitation and told my secretary that he had something important to tell me. But I was in the city, and he went into the air before he had a chance to talk to me. I should say someone murdered him before he could see me."

"What did the police say to that?"

"They never knew about it," Gleason said. "Rogers, our chief test pilot, found the wire and reported to me. We decided to keep it quiet so the man who filed the wire would not be warned and on his guard. We hoped we could catch him ourselves."

"And did you?"

Gleason shook his head. "Not a thing has turned up so far to indicate who he is," he confessed gloomily. "We were still watching when Tom Sullivan was killed."

"And the paper that was missing from your desk drawer?"

"In the excitement of Sullivan's death I paid no attention to my desk drawer.

"And after making certain that the safe was all right, it seemed obvious that nothing had been taken. I didn't miss the paper until the next morning. It was part of the drawing of a wing section," said Gleason crisply. "For a year and a half we have been experimenting toward a new high speed transport type of plane. Air schedules have been too slow.

"Our big transport lines have been dreaming of dawn to dusk transcontinental flights made on schedule with speed and power to take care of emergencies."

"And that," said I, "would be *some* flying."

Gleason nodded. "It would. The manufacturer who can first give them a plane with that performance will reap a rich harvest in prestige and orders, not to speak of the possibilities of converting the design into a long distance army bomber which stands an excellent chance of getting fat government contracts."

Gleason was right. I could understand the enthusiasm

which crept into his voice. Re-design his commercial ship to military specifications, replace the passenger load with bombs, retain speed and long distance performance, and he'd have something the army and navy could use a lot of. I said as much.

"How long," I said, "is it going to take you to get all this?"

"We've got it!" Gleason floored me. "It took a new type wing to give us high speed performance with low landing speed. We've worked in secret, trying to get the jump on everyone else. Not half a dozen people in the factory know what we've been shooting at."

Gleason's lips snapped together. He scowled over the steering wheel at the trees of Lincoln Park which we were skirting.

"That drawing that was stolen out of my desk was the master drawing of part of the section of our new wing. The most unimportant part, thank heaven. But enough to be dangerous if it gets in the wrong hands."

"And my dear chap," said I, remembering to go British for a sentence, "you can lay a quid against a shilling that it's in the wrong hands already. That's the answer. Someone's on to you. They're trying to beat you to the gun. Your killer was in that hall with your office and the plans in mind. He put the watchman out of the way, got what he wanted—and now he's all ready to move after the rest of it."

"That's what I'm afraid of," Gleason rapped out. "I'm convinced Art Ahern wanted to warn me of something like that before he was killed. I don't know what's ahead. But someone is working against the interests of the Gleason Company. They've killed twice—and what will they do next?"

"Nothing, let's hope," I said. "No crook is clever enough to cover his tracks all the time. If he's still around, the job will be that much simpler. But I'll not be working in your factory. I suggest you let me plant someone there."

"Your Chicago office has already done so," Gleason told me. "I believe they're sending a second operative today also. I'll probably see him when I get back to my office. I'll drop you at the house, and while you're getting settled I'll step over to the factory and check up."

"Fine," says I. "And before the day is over I'd like to see these two and have a talk with them."

"You shall." Gleason promised.

3

TENSE UNDERCURRENTS

WINSTEAD, WHERE THE Gleason factory was located, was far out on the north shore, beyond Evanston. It was a small place, but half an eye could see it was lively at this time of the year. The small cottages of the summer people were scattered up and down the lake shore. I saw bathers on a good beach.

The Gleason factory was a collection of ivy-covered, single story buildings lying beside a great flying field, smooth, grass carpeted. Behind the buildings, across a road which skirted the lake, was another narrow grassway extending to the beach, not more than a hundred yards away.

There was a big sheltered cove here on the lake shore, protected by two outstretching necks of land that narrowed in toward each other at their outer point. I caught a glimpse of the end of a pleasure pier farther on. Gleason told me there was a boat pier also, and that the cove had depth enough for yachts and sizable craft to come in and dock.

The older section of the town, near the Gleason factory, had some fine old brick and frame houses. There were large beautiful lawns and big shade trees everywhere.

Gleason's house was a short distance beyond the factory,

and as he wheeled the car up the gravel driveway to the big brick house I could understand why he was content to live in the country when so near the city. Here were leisurely ease and beauty for his spare hours, with sunlight, open air, and plenty of blue sky for the Gleason planes and factory workers.

Gleason stopped the car under a side porte-cochère. A door opened and a woman hastened out.

Gleason said under his breath: "This is my sister Kitty. She is rather hipped on anything British. Watch your step."

We stepped out. Gleason introduced me to Kitty without batting an eyelash. "My dear, may I present my old friend, Cecil Wormley-Squires? My sister, Mrs. Page, Cecil."

Kitty was a thin, nervous little woman, with a shrill, eager voice, a sharp, inquisitive nose and a burbling effervescent manner that pounced on me like a victim tied and tagged for her own use.

"Mr. Wormley-Squires, I am so happy to have you with us!" Kitty burbled, clutching my hand and giving me the once over with her bright little eyes. "Of course Winstead is nothing like Chicago or London, but I hope you do enjoy your stay. I try to make dear Wilbur's house as much like a restful English manor as possible. And I'm sure it's going to be such fun talking over England and the Continent with you. Stanley, my husband, and I haven't been able to get across for three years."

And while Gleason watched with an ironic twinkle in his eye I bowed over Kitty's hand and assured her with a grade A accent: "Charming of you to say so, my deah Mrs. Page. I expect to enjoy myself no end. So restful and quiet after London, eh? Uh—our Sussex place has been closed for some time, and we have been staying in the city. Frightful bore at times, don't you think?"

"I do indeed," Kitty shrilled. "That is why Stanley and I prefer it here with Wilbur. Without a wife he gets so lonesome, and I like to feel that Stanley and I are helping him in our small way. I do hope you like bridge, Mr. Wormley-Squires. We keep open house here and play a great deal."

"Delightful," I murmured, and cursed the little lady under my breath as she led us into the house, still talking.

I could play bridge when I was blackjacked into it, but I hated the game. And I had been delivered into the clutches of a bridge fiend.

A SERVANT BROUGHT my bags in. Gleason said he'd run along. Kitty showed me to my room on the north side of the second floor. She said they were playing bridge downstairs and I must join them as soon as I was rested and had made myself at home.

"We try to keep the informal atmosphere of an English week-end," Kitty said brightly. "Our guests do as they wish at all times. So *do* feel free to please yourself, Mr. Wormley-Squires."

"I shall, dear Mrs. Page," I yearned at her, and made my own private reservations. Everyone about the house was evidently free to do as he pleased but poor Wilbur, who had to keep his nose to the grindstone. I had heard the murmur of a large group in the front of the house as we came upstairs. Kitty, by all the signs, was social and working hard at it.

So after a bath and change I found the back stairs and

slipped out before Kitty's eagle eye could spot me. I walked to the Gleason factory and strayed into the entrance hall of the office building.

A girl was there at a desk, and beside it stood a plump, bustling, partly-bald man wearing pince-nez. I saw his eyes covertly slide to me. I saw him go still and listen as I said to the girl in my best over-the-water accent: "Mr. Wormley-Squires to see Mr. Gleason."

His head jerked around and so did he. A greeter's smile spread over his face. A hand closed over mine before I had anything to say about it.

"Mr. Gleason is expecting you, Mr. Wormley-Squires," he beamed. "I am Hall, the factory manager. Just over from England, I understand." And he pumped my fist like a poor relative with an eye on the will.

"Just over from England," I agreed. "How d'y'do?" And as I salvaged my mitt I got the feeling that Hall had been hanging around waiting for me to turn up. Waiting for his own personal eyeful. The toothy smile, the hand that grabbed for mine were just a shade too enthusiastic to be the real McCoy.

And then and there I put Hall down for future notice. Despite his bald head, his plump face and dignified glasses he looked like a smooth one, a smart one. His next question sounded like it had a hook on it.

"You'll be wanting to go through the factory and look into everything," Hall suggested—and watched me intently through his pince-nez.

I batted my eyes, nodded indifferently.

"Before I leave. Int'r'sted in all this, y'know. Looking for new ideas, and all that."

Hall passed a moist palm over his bald spot, nodded, smiled. "Of course. Mr. Gleason has told me of your interest in aeronautics. Perhaps we can give you a few new ideas."

And I wondered what the devil he meant by that as the girl put down the telephone and gave me the welcome sign.

"Go right in, Mr. Wormley-Squires," she cooed. "Mr. Gleason is not in his office at the moment, but the girl will get him for you. Through that door to your right."

So I let Hall pilot me through that door and turn me to the right, where a door at the end of the hall was lettered, MR. GLEASON. And a glance back at the desk showed the girl staring after me with a queer look on her face. She had lost her smile. She looked thoughtful, expectant. Come to think of it the same look had been on her face when I walked in. There was bustle, movement, work all through the factory, but there was also a strained undercurrent in the atmosphere. I had seen it in a hundred other places where murder and crookedness had been done. It was always the same. I could sense it without looking. Behind the everyday exterior that greeted the casual eye one found a furtive tenseness, waiting for something to happen. It was here in the Gleason factory.

Hall went one way, and I went through Gleason's door into a waiting room where a girl was banging busily on a typewriter. Without looking up or stopping the clatter of her machine, she said: "Sit down, Ape. The boss will be along in a few minutes."

I gagged, dropped a breath, yelped: "Trixie! What the— the—"

"Don't swallow your bridgework, Ape," Trixie advised

tartly as she looked up from the machine and eyed me through a pair of horn-rimmed glasses.

4

A SUSPICIOUS EAVESDROPPER

YES, IT WAS little Trixie Meehan, who had her knife out
and her tongue sharpened for me from London to Shang-
hai. And what a tongue! What a girl! When we parted
down in Florida after a hair raising case it had been with
the mutual wish that one or the other would get run over
by a coal truck before our paths crossed again. Trixie had
told me too much about myself just before that.

What a girl!—for someone else.

But in case you've never met Trixie Meehan, get her
right from her severest critic. When they made a woman
detective out of Trixie and gave her to the Blaine Agency
they broke the mold and buried the parts. Trixie had it all.

She thought so fast it made me dizzy at times. Yes, me,
hard boiled Mike Harris, who was supposed to be an ace.
And with all that, Trixie had It, and If, and Then and Those.

I was a half pint, and proud of it. But Trixie was a quarter
pint, who could knock 'em dizzy with one look out of her
big soft eyes. I know. She had knocked me dizzy the first
time we met, and while I was still too dizzy to call my plays
she knocked me groggy with a right hand smack and laid
down the law. Looks were free—but no sampling.

Trixie was little, frail, soft, with a wistful, helpless

manner that wrecked big rough men and fooled a lot of women. But when you walked around behind that, you ran into a tongue that could take the hide off a stuffed moose, muscles that were steel, and endurance and reckless courage that kept my heart in my mouth when we got into tight spots together.

Trixie was the hardest, toughest case in the whole world-wide Blaine organization. She had been everywhere and done everything. She was their ace woman operative, and somehow we were always being thrown on cases together. Sometimes I thought Trixie asked for them, but I never could prove it. Out of a hundred and twenty million people she singled me out to pick on. When it wasn't to my face, she spent her time going around the country dressing up my reputation to suit herself.

And here she was behind Gleason's typewriter, with fake horn-rimmed glasses, hair slicked back tight and severe from her face, and a plain black business dress that made her look almost dowdy, if one neglected to examine the curves underneath.

"Who let you in here?" I snarled. "I thought you were heading out to Frisco."

Trixie smiled sweetly.

"I was, but they sidetracked me to Chicago. And that nice Mr. Carston, in the Chicago office, assigned me out here."

"You mean you asked for it when you heard I was coming!" I snapped, glaring at her.

"Guilty," Trixie admitted without shame. "I wanted to see what sort of an ass you'd be with a name like Wormley-Squires. Go into your act, Ape. Let's see what you've got on the ball."

"This is too much!" I choked. "Scram back to the office and tell them to send out someone I can get along with. I'm running this job, and I'll have none of your wisecracking at my neck. This is serious business. There's a killer running around loose here. If he ever finds out you're after him, you may get a knife in your back like that night watchman did!"

"I believe the man is really worried about little Trixie's health," she dimpled at me.

"Bah!" says I weakly, for Trixie had taken off her glasses and was giving me one of those wistful appealing looks I never could stay strong under.

Trixie sighed and looked about twelve years old.

"I was really afraid you'd get into trouble yourself, Ape," she said wistfully. "So I came out here to save you."

"Rats!" I said, weaker.

"That's my story and I'll stick to it," Trixie stated with a determined nod of her little head. "But if it doesn't suit you, let me break the sad news. You haven't a blasted thing to do with it, Mike Harris. Carston assured me I was on the job until the end. So take it and like it, and stop getting red in the face."

And at that moment I saw a faint shadow flick for an instant across one corner of the opaque door glass. I gave Trixie my back, reached the door with noiseless steps and yanked it open.

And grabbed the arm of a thin, gangling young man standing outside and yanked him in.

"Percy!" Trixie exclaimed, jumping up.

Percy looked about sixteen. His hair needed cutting, and there was a sly smart look behind his fright.

"Young man, what were you doing outside that door?" I demanded sternly.

Percy swallowed, looked from Trixie to me with a guilty, cornered air, and shuffled his feet. "Nothin," he denied, looking down at the floor.

"You were sneaking out there!" Trixie accused.

"Out with it, Percy," I said. "Who put you up to it?"

Percy looked startled. He reddened. And then sly stubbornness glinted in his eyes. "Miss Malone sent me to collect the mail," he mumbled. "I heard someone talkin' in here an' thought I'd wait."

"You don't usually wait!" Trixie snapped.

Percy dug a toe into the rug and looked at Trixie defiantly. "Well, I was waitin' this time," he muttered.

"Who is Miss Malone?" I asked Trixie.

"Mr. Hall's secretary."

"Well, well, well," I said softly. "Percy, what did you hear while you were standing outside there?"

"Nothin'," Percy denied.

And there didn't seem to be any use in firing questions at him. Trixie gave him a couple of letters and Percy left hurriedly with obvious relief.

Trixie and I looked at each other.

"I wonder what he heard?" I said.

TRIXIE SHRUGGED HER little shoulders regretfully. "I don't know. We were both talking louder than we should."

"I was talking to Hall just before I came in here. How about this Malone woman?"

"Sweet on Hall," Trixie said promptly. "And smart."

"Hall put her up to it," I decided with a frown. "Got a line on him?"

"Not much," Trixie admitted. "I only came here yesterday. He seems to be a good factory manager. A fiend for detail and able to get a lot of work out of the force. Don't let his looks fool you. I get the idea that half the factory is afraid of him. Terrible temper, and not averse to using it. And a hard worker. Days, nights and holidays he's apt to be around here."

"Nights, eh?" I said under my breath. "That is interesting."

And the door opened and Gleason walked in. His face lit up at sight of me. "Ah, glad to see you got over so quick," he said briskly. "I see you two have been talking. Do you know each other?"

That reminded me Trixie and I had a feud on. "We've met," I admitted sourly.

"Good. Miss Meehan is one of the two operatives the Chicago office sent out. I've put her in my office here; and arranged it so she has ready access to all parts of the factory. I'm in hopes that, getting about with her eyes and ears open, she may uncover something that would be hidden to the rest of us."

"Undoubtedly," I agreed. "Miss Meehan can uncover things you never suspected. But has it occurred to you, Mr. Gleason, that if her identity is discovered, something might happen to her?"

Gleason frowned. Then shrugged. "Frankly, it has not. But I suppose such hazards go with the work. Miss Meehan is free to leave when she desires."

"She doesn't desire," Trixie said flatly.

And that was that. I made the best of a bad bargain and asked her, for my benefit and Gleason's: "Have you uncovered anything yet?"

"No," Trixie admitted. "But I only came yesterday. Give me time."

"What can you tell me about Hall, your factory manager?" I asked Gleason. "Met him when I came in."

"A good man," Gleason said promptly. "Hard worker and knows the business straight through. He's a technical man and a practical one, too. Frankly, it would be hard to get along without him."

"Trust him?"

"Absolutely." Gleason smiled at the idea. "He wouldn't be where he is now if I didn't," he pointed out.

Gleason glanced at his wrist watch.

"Three-thirty. We're having a test flight at four to get some data on a new model. Walk out with me and have a look."

And I went, unsuspecting the horror we were walking into.

Gleason led me through a couple of the factory buildings. He had a fine layout, a busy force of workers, and every sign pointed to a successful business. But as we walked through those workers a wave of interest seemed to run before us. Eyes watched us. Heads turned. Furtive remarks passed from mouth to mouth. I recognized that undercurrent I had spotted in the front offices.

We came out into the bright sunshine, with the great flat flying field to our left and the factory buildings stretching ahead of it.

"The new model is in that end hangar," Gleason pointed

out. "And here comes Sam Davis, who's going to take her up. Fine boy. Over four thousand hours on his ticket, and what he doesn't know about planes isn't worth mentioning. I place him next to Rogers, our chief pilot. He—er—took Art Ahern's place."

Sam Davis, turning away from an overalled companion who walked on toward the end hangar, was in his middle twenties, wiry, quick-moving and alert, even with his chute pack hanging heavily behind him.

He carried a leather helmet and goggles in one hand, and had a grim and firm handshake for me when Gleason introduced us.

"All ready to go up?" Gleason asked.

"Just heading for the hangar when I saw you coming," Davis stated. "Brown and I have been working since lunch on the motor. I had an idea a little different gas feed might get a few more miles an hour. It's a sweet looking job, Mr. Gleason. I'm keen to get it in the air."

"So am I," Gleason nodded. "I need the test figures tonight. Want to go over them before morning. We've got some new ideas in that plane we're using on those big transport models. Check your take-off and landing speeds very close, and your maximum and cruising air speeds."

"I'll do that," Davis agreed as we strolled toward the hangar whose wide, corrugated doors were rolled down.

Queer how things happen. I was not even looking at the hangar when Sam Davis burst out: "What's the matter with Brown?" At the same instant a strangled, bubbling, unearthly scream reached our ears.

5

DEATH AND A BURNING SHIP

I JERKED MY head up and looked toward the hangar, where that scream had sounded. And to my dying day I'll never forget what I saw.

There was a small door beside the wide metal curtain that formed the main door of the hangar. That smaller door had opened. Brown, the mechanic who had entered the hangar a few moments before, had lunged out.

Brown had screamed. Brown was staggering through the warm sunlight toward us, with both hands clutched at his throat. He was less than a hundred yards away. I could see the contorted agony of his pale face, eyes fairly starting from their sockets.

All three of us broke into a run. And Brown screamed again, weaker, but with a spine-chilling note of terror. His hands came away from his throat. For an instant I saw the long, thin blade of a knife silhouetted in the air, and the sickening gush of blood that welled down over his chest.

I knew then what we were seeing. A man dying. And before Brown lurched three more steps he went forward on his face, rolled to his side, his back. When we reached him he was spread-eagled on the ground, the knife still in his fingers, gasping faintly, staring up at the high blue sky from wide, fixed eyes.

Sam Davis went down on his knees, dropping goggles and leather helmet unheedingly. "Brown!" he demanded wildly. "What happened?"

Brown's eyes did not turn toward him. I think that Brown did not even know we were there. I think he was a dead man when he came out of that hangar door, staggering, lurching into space for the help he was never to get in this life.

Gleason, too, bent over the prone figure. "Brown, can you hear me?" he begged.

But Brown lay there with his torn throat, staring at the deep blue sky. A dying man watching the sky. Perhaps Brown already knew what lay in that vast blue vault above.

I let them waste their words and sprinted toward the hangar. The answer to this ghastly mystery lay in there. The small door was standing open as Brown had left it. I noted patches of fresh bright blood on the sill, on the door itself as I plunged into the big, shadowy interior of the hangar.

Three planes stood in the hangar, one facing the big door; and that seemed all. It was deserted of life. My shoes scraped loudly on the cement floor as I ran forward. The blood led to the first machine, a high-winged, single motor transport job. And the grisly death trail ended there beside it, at the rear edge of the wing. Drops of blood coming to an abrupt end! There Brown had stood when the knife had been driven into his throat!

I went behind the plane, searching every spot where a man might be lurking. But I knew it was useless as I went. And I was right. There was no man in the hangar. Work benches stood along the opposite side, and a door was set at the back on that side.

A door. I knew then where the killer had gone. But when I ran through it into the sunlight once more, I drew blank. There was no one in sight. This was the end building. There were shrubs and trees about, and a board fence less than twenty paces away. It was a blind spot on the property. A man could move here with little chance of being seen by anyone. A man *had* moved here!

I ran to the fence, drew myself up, looked on the other side. A cindered alleyway ran there, one way to the street, the other back to the intersecting alley behind the adjoining houses. No one was in sight there. The killer could have gone any one of three ways, to the street, the rear alley, or back behind the hangar to the other factory buildings.

I ran back to the intersecting alley and found nothing. The killer had vanished. He would have to be traced, some other way. I re-scaled the fence and returned to the front of the hangar.

Brown lay dead. Several excited workmen had hastened to the spot and were staring curiously. Gleason had followed me into the hangar and was just coming out. He looked stricken, grave, as we met at the body. Sam Davis was there with a white, set face, and standing beside him was a tall, well dressed stranger.

"He's dead!" Sam Davis said to me in a tight voice. "He was joking just before he left me. Now look at him! Dead! Murdered!"

An excited murmur came from the workmen. The tall stranger shook his head regretfully, raised tapering fingers to his cravat and adjusted it mechanically. "Frightful bit of business," he said unsteadily.

Gleason introduced me to him briefly: "My brother-in-law, Mr. Stanley Page. Mr. Wormley-Squires, our guest from England."

There was little time to note such things, but I could not help seeing that Stanley Page might have been turned out by a Bond Street tailor. He had that graceful, urbane, assured air of the sophisticated. His hair was brushed back in a correct sweep. His face was lean and good looking. And his glance was open, frank, friendly.

"I'm sorry your visit has to be opened by a tragedy like this," he told me, and shook his head again.

GLEASON LOOKED INQUIRINGLY at me, an unspoken question in his eyes.

I shook my head. "Nothing in the hangar. I went out the rear door. No one in sight there." I turned to the men. "Scatter out and question everyone in the factory who might have seen some one running behind that hangar. And some one telephone the police."

They went, looking back over their shoulders.

"This is pretty ghastly!" Gleason said in a low voice.

"Worse than that," I agreed. "This man found someone in the hangar when he went in. Who was supposed to be in there?"

"No one!" Sam Davis jerked out. "We were working in there alone all afternoon. When we finished and I went to get my flying togs, Brown went along. I supposed the hangar was empty when he went back in."

I looked down at the lax form at our feet. "If he could speak one word. He knew the man he found in there. Knew him well enough to let him get close enough to use that knife. He was killed by a man he thought was his friend."

Gleason passed a hand over his chin, thumb brushing his lips, and turned a meaning look on me. "Like—"

"Like your night watchman," I finished for him. "Same method. Same man, I'd say."

Stanley Page stooped, pulled the knife from the dead man's fingers before I could stop him.

"Put it down! You'll ruin any possible finger prints!" I burst out.

He dropped the knife, smiled apologetically. "Sorry. I didn't think. You seem to know a great deal about such things. Do you mean to say that if we find who this knife belongs to, we'll have the man who killed the night watchman some time ago?"

"Absolutely."

Page looked at me admiringly. "Extraordinary! I never would have thought of it. But, gentlemen"—he looked at the three of us and spread his hands, fingers apart—"I can't understand this killing with knives. We can't have a Paris Apache among us. I should think he would use a revolver. This—this sort of thing is—er—hardly sporting."

"I'm afraid, my dear fellow, the sporting element doesn't enter into it," I said dryly. "A shot would have brought us all into that hangar on the run. The man who used that knife probably thought this poor fellow would drop instantly and give him plenty of time to get away. It was mere chance that Brown had the vitality to stagger out the door where we saw him. Using the knife was cold blooded, but clever. Have any of you ever seen it before?"

The weapon had once been a small butcher knife by the

looks of it. The handle was wrapped with black tire tape. The blade, worn down with use, had been honed to a sharp cutting edge and a keen point.

Stanley Page stared down with narrowed eyes at the knife.

"I've been trying to think," he confessed. "It seems to me I've seen knives like that around the factory here. In the fabric room, Wilbur."

Gleason snapped thumb and forefinger excitedly. "I believe you're right! Don't say anything about it. I'll check up and see if there's a knife missing."

Sam Davis had been listening silently. Now he glanced at his wrist watch. "I can't do any good there," he remarked.

"I think I'll get into the air and make my test."

"Don't!" I warned sharply. "Er—none of my business, of course, but the man who was in that hangar was there for a purpose. I understand you've lost one man through sabotage. There may be something wrong with that plane."

Davis slapped helmet and goggles against a leg. His face was drawn, haggard.

"Brown was my friend," he said thickly. "This has hit me pretty hard. I want to get away for a little while. It's lonesome and—and clean up there." He lifted his eyes to the sky for an instant, as if drawing strength from "up there." "I can go over the ship in a few minutes and find out if there's anything wrong," he appealed to Gleason. "And I have my chute. You said you wanted those performance figures this evening."

I could see the struggle taking place in Gleason. "I do," he admitted. "It's up to you, I guess. But go over the ship carefully. We want no more accidents like Ahern had."

"I'll help," Stanley Page offered quickly. "Anything to get my mind off this."

They walked off together, the wiry test pilot with his parachute pack bumping against his legs, and his tall, easy moving companion. Stanley Page was a handsome man, far more likable than his wife, Kitty.

"Does your brother-in-law work here at the factory?" I asked Gleason absently.

"In a manner of speaking. He's flown some, and helps out where he's needed," Gleason said briefly.

And I got the impression he had made a job so Page might draw a salary check without loss of face. The old in-law problem.

We were alone. The corpse lay between us, staring with sightless eyes at the sky. And my last scruples against coming out here to Chicago left me. Death, cold, cruel, vicious, was slinking through the Gleason factory. Death that stalked by night and day, that struck on the ground or in the sky. And strangely, for an instant, my mind flashed to Trixie Meehan, and I wondered what would happen to her.

"This man had no plans to steal," I mused. "You're up against something bigger than you thought."

"I'm afraid so," Gleason said heavily. "I wish the police would get here."

THEY DID, THREE of them in a little touring car. Nice blue uniforms, swanky caps and importance. They were evidently demons when it came to tagging cars of the summer visitors. But they looked dumb for anything like this. They were dumb.

The chief himself was there, a leathery looking oldster by the name of Willis. They looked at the body and conferred.

They asked questions, poked around the hangar, asked more questions of the men I had sent out to question the other factory workers.

No one had seen anything. No one knew anything. And the chief wrapped the knife up carefully in a piece of paper and put it in his pocket. And the coroner came with the undertaker, asked more questions, and they took the body away.

Chief Willis masticated a hunk of gum, shifted from one foot to the other, delivered himself of his conclusions weightily. "It looks like your man was murdered, Mr. Gleason."

I had said nothing. The less they knew, the less they did, the easier it would be for me. I didn't want to be stumbling over them wherever I turned.

Gleason gave me a look of disgust, answered with a shade of irony, "That had occurred to me, Chief. What do you intend to do?"

The Chief shifted his gum to the other side of his face, glanced around with a knowing scowl. "I'm going to have this knife examined for fingerprints, an' try an' find out who was in that hangar. When we know that, we'll have the man who killed him."

"Not a doubt of it," Gleason agreed. "Call on me for any assistance you need. And now will you pardon me? We're sending a plane up."

The door of the hangar had rolled up with a harsh grating sound. Mechanics were wheeling the ship out. And murder went by the board while the Winstead police force adjourned to watch the circus.

Sam Davis was standing to one side with Stanley Page

while the mechanics made ready to start the radial engine. I went over to them.

"Everything all right?" I asked.

Sam Davis nodded. "We didn't find a thing wrong. Controls, guy wires and braces seem to be all right."

Stanley Page turned to Gleason and myself. "Perhaps Mr. Wormley-Squires would like to go up with Davis," he suggested. "Fine chance for a bit of diversion."

Gleason hesitated, and then assented: "Not a bad idea. It's up to our guest."

"Rather," I accepted. "Great chance to see how your American types behave in the air."

Sam Davis broke in curtly, "Not this trip. I never allow anyone in the plane when I'm testing. Too many chances for a bug to crop out and something go wrong."

"He could wear a parachute," Page pointed out. "With a cabin plane of this type there would be a chance to jump if anything went wrong."

"No," said Davis with finality. "I never break that rule. I—I lost a passenger once that way. Never again."

Page turned to his brother-in-law for support. But Gleason shook his head. "Davis has the say so. If he says no, I'm afraid it's no go."

Page smiled apologetically at me. "Sorry, old chap. Some other time perhaps."

And that was that. The motor spun over with a roar. Davis donned helmet and goggles, took a pad of test reports from one of the mechanics, waved his hand at us, and entered the plane. For a few minutes his head and shoulders were visible in the pilot's cockpit behind the silver blur of the propeller while he warmed the engine.

And then with a final wave of his hand he taxied down to the end of the field, gave her the gun, swept forward, took the air smoothly and began to climb in great spirals.

It was a neat six-place cabin job, trim, streamlined, with great speed and climbing performance.

We all stood there in front of the hangar with our heads craned back, murder and violence forgotten for the moment in the splendid sight of that speedy plane boring into the sky. I began to regret that it had not been possible for me to go along.

Davis had two thousand feet over the field, and the silver wings of his plane were getting smaller when a puff of black smoke streamed out just behind the engine. The plane lurched, staggered, tilted over. One wing folded back like a broken arm and the whole front of the plane seemed to burst into a sheet of flame as it went into a vertical dive.

Stanley Page cried out loudly: "Something's wrong! He's burning up!"

6

PYRE OF DEATH

I DID NOT look at Page. Neck craned back until it hurt, I watched a blazing comet whirl into a vertical spin and plunge toward the earth. Down—down—down… No hope of saving it. No one to help young Sam Davis sitting in the heart of that plunging inferno.

A thousand feet were wiped out in seconds. Concerted exclamations of awe burst out around me as a small black object fell from the plane and whirled over and over in the air. A cloud of white silk blossomed over it. The plane fell on alone, crashed into the flying field a quarter of a mile away and burst into a fountain of fire. And Sam Davis drifted down slowly, hauling on the shroud lines to guide his descent.

Gleason uttered a husky: "Thank God! The boy's all right!"

And Stanley Page said hoarsely: "He must have acted quick to get out like that."

Gleason was pale. Page looked like a ghost, his mouth working, his tapering fingers digging into his palms as we all ran out toward the spot where Sam Davis was landing.

Davis struck the ground hard, was dragged a few yards until he managed to collapse the chute. His face was a

smear of black oil as he unsnapped the chute harness
and turned to meet us, limping slightly. But he was calm.
Calmer than any of us in the face of that crackling pyre of
death not far away. I felt a cold chill crawl down my back as
I looked over there. By the merest chance I had escaped it.

"What happened?" Gleason demanded harshly.

Sam Davis ran a handkerchief over his oily features and
shrugged. "Can't tell you, Mr. Gleason. Everything was
clicking perfectly when something seemed to explode just
back of me. It knocked me groggy, but I had sense enough
left to realize one of the wing tanks had been ruptured and
gasoline was sheeting over everything. I knew I'd have fire
in a few seconds so I ducked back into the cabin, fought
my way to the door, managed to get it open against the air
pressure and bailed out. Everything was black by then and
fire seemed to be all around me. I was blank, but I managed
to find the cord and yank it. And my head cleared before
I reached the ground."

Davis grinned thinly at me. "Good thing you didn't go
up."

"An explosion!" Gleason exclaimed. His face settled into
a thoughtful mask. "Any idea what caused it?"

Davis started to say something, then closed his lips
firmly and shook his head. "No," he denied. "I had no warning. I wasn't much good for thinking directly after. Perhaps
a spark got to a gas line."

And I had the feeling Davis suspected more than he was
telling. But with strangers crowding around I let it wait. It
was quitting time. Half the factory force had swarmed out
on the field and were streaming toward us. At the burning

plane several men were making ineffectual efforts with fire extinguishers.

"Everything looked all right before he went up," Page declared excitedly.

Davis agreed with him. "As far as I could see, it was," he said.

Gleason suddenly looked weary, haggard, tired. His eyes strayed to the wrecked plane. His shoulders sagged. But he uttered no word of complaint.

"Thank heaven you got out all right," was all he said. "There's nothing more we can do here. Go to your doctor for an examination, and then home for a rest, Davis. I'll talk to you tomorrow. Er—Cecil, coming with me?"

Stanley Page fell in with us. "I'm tired, Stan," Gleason said to him. "Will you please get that wreck in the hangar before you go home?"

Page said with a willing smile, "Not at all, old chap." And turned back.

GLEASON NODDED TO some of the workers we passed. They were serious, troubled. Far more so than should have been the case over one plane accident. Plainly their morale was getting in a serious condition. Gleason was silent for some moments. When he spoke his voice was heavy, puzzled.

"Gasoline lines back in the wing don't break and explode. If it had been fire around the motor first, yes. But that explosion wasn't at the motor. The wing started to give at once."

"Any ideas?"

"No," said Gleason. "But I don't think it was an accident."

And we met Trixie, hurrying out from the offices. Her eyes questioned me. "Another accident," I said. "And a murder just before that. Where's Hall?"

"He and his secretary rode off twenty minutes ago," Trixie said. "If you have nothing more for me to do I think I'll mix with the crowd, Mr. Gleason."

"Just a minute," I said. "Where's his other operative?"

Trixie looked at me with dancing devils in her eyes. "He's the new night watchman," she said calmly. "Mr. Hall employed him yesterday without knowing who he was."

Gleason looked chagrined. "I had no idea," he confessed. "Been expecting a man all day. I suppose your agency had a reason."

"Probably," Trixie agreed demurely, and before Gleason's eyes she calmly handed me a slip of paper and went her way. I read her address.

Gleason made no comment about it. He was in a black study as we walked toward his house. A badly worried man. He spoke abruptly, passing a hand wearily over his eyes.

"I'm going to be frank with you—er—Squires, because you seem to be the only one who can help me now. Business has been bad for two years. I've borrowed all I can. New contracts mean new models. I've called workers back recently, scraped together all possible money, and staked everything on the new design. It means success if I put it over. Bankruptcy if I fail. Two of our test planes have smashed up. The American Air Lines are holding tests now with the idea of replacing their whole fleet. That contract would save me. I can't get it with paper plans. I've been asking them to hold off any decision until I can show them the new Gleason transport. They won't wait much longer."

Gleason passed his hand over his eyes again wearily. "I'm being hamstrung on every side. Plans missing. Test planes crashing before I can get their performance figures. The morale of my workers is going fast in the face of sabotage and deliberate murder. This accident today has about put me at the end of my rope. I have a few more orders for light planes to get out, and enough resources to finish the first of the big new transports, if I dispense with the tests I wanted for safety's sake. I have faith enough in the new design to feel certain it will live up to its paper figures. But if anything happens to that big ship when it goes into the air, I'm finished.

"I won't be able to build another—and it will probably be too late to get the American Air Lines contract anyway."

"When will it be ready for a test?" I asked.

"About four more days of rush work."

"Haven't you an idea who could be after your scalp?" I urged.

"No," Gleason denied despairingly. "I've wondered if someone on the payroll isn't working for a competitor. But this is a clean game. I can't think it of any of them."

I said nothing. What was the use of telling Gleason that time after time I had found rottenness in the most unlikely places. Money, love, revenge, envy, all turned up their crimes. People killed more often from panic than cold blooded design. Gleason's night watchman, for instance. Murder probably had been the last thing in the mind of that killer, until panic guided the knife. Desperation over that would make a second murder easier than the first.

I wondered where Hall, the factory manager, had been when the mechanic was killed in the hangar. Why had Hall left so soon after with this Miss Malone, who had sent the office boy to spy on me?

Was it possible Hall was trying to wreck the factory he managed, with an eye to a bankruptcy sale. I was beginning to believe anything might be possible in this peaceful little community of Winstead; and I put Hall down for close attention.

KITTY PAGE AND her guests had heard the news and were all a-twitter. Yes, there were still guests, for dinner, and bridge afterwards. Ten of them—on Gleason's money. Kitty's guests. Gleason wandered about his own house like a boarder.

I donned white flannels and a blue coat for dinner. Page turned up with his winning smile and impeccable manners in time to join us. He answered questions good-naturedly, and now and then grew grave as his mind seemed to wander back to the late tragedy.

I heard him say to Gleason: "We ran a fire hose out to it, cooled everything off, and got the mess in the hangar."

"Any indication of what happened?" Gleason questioned.

Stanley Page shook his head. "Not a thing, Wilbur. It must have been something in the gas line."

"I'll go back this evening and look at it," Gleason said. And once more I caught a note of near defeat in his voice.

Kitty Page's high shrill chatter dominated the dinner table. Gleason sat at one end, smiling faintly now and then, but hardly speaking. Stanley Page devoted himself to the girl at his right, a young beauty. She was on my left, but he hardly let her have a word with me. His line was a good one, I had to admit.

Kitty's eyes rested on him now and then. Distinctly not love glances. Her "dear Stanley" was plainly in bad. After dinner I had a cigar with the men for politeness, and then drew Gleason aside.

"I'm going out," I said.

"Quite all right. Any specific purpose?"

"No," I parried. "Have you a car I can use?"

"Take the green roadster."

So I drove off in Gleason's car. It was dark. The summer colony was out in force. The pleasure pier was festooned with lights. A band was playing. Couples were dancing on an open dance floor. Murder, mystery, sudden death seemed very remote from these summer delights.

From a drug store I got Hall's address. He lived down near the other end of town in a small cottage alone. The house was dark when I drove up. The people next door were on their front porch. From them I learned that Hall had driven off just before dark with a young woman companion. No, he had taken no suit cases. His car was a blue coupé. I left with a feeling of relief. It had occurred to me that Hall might have skipped town.

I looked for them along the beach front. They were not there. So I climbed into the green roadster and idled north out of town to think things over.

A sedan going fast passed me about two miles out. It lurched off the road a quarter of a mile ahead and came to an abrupt stop with head lights glaring into a weed bordered fence. When I reached the spot a man was standing in the road waving his arms.

I stopped. Who wouldn't?

"Something wrong?" I asked, as he came to the side of the car.

"The steering gear. I—I'm afraid my wife is badly hurt!" he gasped. "Help me get her out and back to a doctor, please!"

In the darkness I could barely see that he was short, thin, with a wizened face under the brim of a Panama hat. I jumped out and went over to the car with him. He opened the rear door instead of the front.

And something clipped me back of the ear neatly. Groggy, half out, I pitched forward in the car as he shoved hard on my back.

7

SLATED FOR DEATH

THERE WERE TWO of them, one lurking in the car. He pounced on me before I hit the floor, driving his knees into my back, pinning me down.

I lay doggo. It wasn't hard. I was half unconscious, sick, weak, and everything was spinning. They talked as they searched me.

"That was a dirty one, Harry. You knocked him cold."

"Good enough for him, the lousy dick! I hope I busted his head open!"

I almost grunted with surprise. All the elaborate camouflage had done no good. Someone beside Gleason knew who I was. Gleason had told no one, not even his household. It traced directly back to Hall, his secretary and the office boy who had listened while I talked to Trixie. And I went cold, thinking of Trixie Meehan. If they knew me, they knew her. If this had happened to me, she could expect little better. And she was not warned.

I had a gun under my armpit. Never went out without one. They found it.

"All ready for trouble!" the wizened one who had decoyed me sneered.

"He's found it," the other one grunted. "Help me get him back in his car."

I held my breath, kept my eyes closed while they hauled me out on the ground like a sack of potatoes. They lifted me by ankles and shoulders and dumped me in the green roadster. One of them got in behind the wheel, the wizened one, for his companion spoke over the door at my side.

"Here's the booze. Put it in the door pocket. I'll stop at the turn-off. Crack him again just before you get to the quarry, and then run him in. And make sure he don't come out of it before you get there."

"I'll plug him if he does!" Harry, the wizened one, snarled.

"Don't try anything like that, you fool! This has got to be an accident. A bullet hole and a lot of blood will crab that. Just crack him."

"All right, I'll crack him!" Harry agreed—and he sounded reluctant, the little swine.

I had no illusions by then. These two were killers, and Mike Harris was slated to be on the victim's end. It was a smooth idea. Somewhere nearby was a quarry. Car, Mike Harris and all were to be run into the quarry. It might be weeks before I was found. And then, with nothing but a bump or two on my head and a bottle of booze on the seat beside me, it would be a plain case of drunken driving in strange country.

The green roadster rolled on down the road.

They had jammed me down in front of the seat, with the back of my head resting against the seat edge. I was invisible from the road there, and I couldn't move without the man behind the wheel spotting me instantly and going into action.

I spent half the first mile silently swearing at myself for walking into the trap, and trying to get my head cleared and my strength back. And the next mile trying to see a way out of it. I was not armed and the man behind the wheel was. He could—and would—drop me the instant I moved. My cramped legs were beginning to go numb. It was a mess, but I had been in tighter places.

He drove fast, turned off the road in about five minutes. The car bounced, swayed over an uneven road. And I knew the end was not far off now.

I had my eyes open by then. By the dashlight glow I could see the driver's legs and feet. His dark trousers were creased to a knife edge, his shoes were fancy black and white leather. Dressed for a party and making it a killing.

His foot came off the accelerator and went to the brake while the other pushed the clutch in. The car swung to the right. And I knew we had come to the jumping off place. His hands, feet and eyes were busy just then. I jabbed up an arm and brought it down against his chest.

He cursed loudly. The car stopped with a jerk as he jammed his foot hard on the brake. By then I had a grip on his coat lapel and was coming up off the floor. He tried to knock me back; but he was jammed in behind the steering wheel and my arm was across his body, blocking his arms for a moment. A big man would have gotten all tangled up in that cramped space. I lunged up off the floor and drove against him before he knew what was happening.

A GUN LAY on the seat beside a whiskey bottle. He tried to grab for it. I knocked the arm back, drove a savage looping hook over the steering wheel rim into his face. His head slammed back against the seat, hat falling off, nose flattening, blood spurting. His nose would never be the same again.

I threw myself on the seat, over the gun, and jammed him back into the corner behind the wheel, smashing him in the face again. The top was down, there was plenty of room for action. He slid down under me, reaching for the gun. I tried to block his arm, and grabbed for it myself. And suddenly he was out from behind the wheel, sliding down over the running board. He had opened the door, wriggled under the wheel and out.

His steps raced to the back of the car and kept going. I got the gun, stood up in the seat. And he fired out of the darkness, a licking spit of flame, a crashing report. Windshield glass shattered behind me.

I snapped off the lights and vaulted out of the car as he shot twice more. How near he came to me I didn't know until later when I found a bullet hole through the side of my coat. From the ground I shot twice toward him. No more answered. He had vanished in the blackness back there. Listening, with the ring of gunfire in my ears, I heard his steps running back along the road. I followed.

There was a turn. A hundred yards beyond it headlights snapped on. A door slammed. The car rushed off in low gear, leaving me standing in the road swearing.

I saw them turn into the main highway just beyond and race back toward Winstead. And I ran for the green roadster.

The place was silent, deserted, with no houses near. When I turned the headlights on again they stabbed over into space. Standing on the seat I looked far down at the still gleam of water.

We had halted at the very edge of an old quarry. And I admit to a chill as I thought of what might have happened.

Drops of fresh blood dotted the steering wheel. The gun on the seat had been mine. The whiskey bottle was half empty.

Anyone finding it would not have wondered why the car was in the quarry.

I had a Panama hat and a whiskey bottle for clues as I sent the big roadster rocketing back toward Winstead. But that was all. I doubted if I would recognize the little man again. At no time had I seen his face clearly, or his companion at all. I was not even sure what color their car was, let alone the make.

They got away, losing themselves in Winstead, or keeping on for all I knew. I hunted up the Lakeside Apartments, a four-story jerry-built stucco, found Trixie's card in a mail box as if she intended to stay permanently, hurried to the rear of the first floor and hammered on her door.

Trixie opened it at once. "What's the idea of trying to break the door down?" she demanded tartly. And then her eyes widened and she exclaimed:

"There's blood on your shoulder! What happened?"

I was so relieved to see her all right that I didn't even try to wisecrack as I entered her apartment. "They're wise to us," I said, and told her what had happened to me. "I was afraid they had gotten to you first," I finished.

"Why, Mike, I believe you were really worried about me," Trixie cried. There was a funny look in her eyes. Her face had paled when I told her about my little ride, and now it was pink.

"Why shouldn't I worry about you?" says I crossly. "I need you here on the job. I don't like to change horses in midstream."

"It would have been a good thing if they had dumped you over into that quarry!" Trixie snapped.

And I spent the next five minutes wondering what was the matter with her. Women were a mystery to me. "Get your hat on and take a ride with me," I said finally. "Bring your gun, just in case."

While Trixie went for her hat I found the address I wanted in her telephone book. We parked across the street from a row of bungalows near the beach. It was dark, comfortable, quiet.

"Miss Malone lives across the street there," I said. "Her house is dark. Still out with Hall, I guess. I want to see 'em when they come back. He'll go in and talk with her, and maybe I can get an earful through a window. What kind of a dame is she?"

"A hussy," Trixie said promptly. "Too pretty to be a private secretary. She should be in a chorus. Hall looks at her like a sap. You should have seen him put her into his car outside the factory this afternoon. And she looked at him like he was a knight in shining armor."

"Both that way, eh?" I said cynically. "Well, they say love makes the wheels go around. I'd like to know what it's making go around in this case."

"You don't know anything about love!" Trixie snapped.

And we spent a pleasant fifteen minutes jawing back and forth. What a tongue that girl had! We broke it off as a car rolled up and stopped before Miss Malone's house. It was a coupé.

Voices murmured for a moment. A woman laughed softly. I could see them together inside. They clinched and then got out and went to the house. A moment later the man came back to the machine and drove off. Lights switched on in the house and I said disgustedly: "What kind of a man is he, walking off from a cutie that way?"

"You should know!" Trixie said viciously. "Now that you've wasted half an hour on this, take me back and run on about your business."

My hand was on the ignition key when I drew back and watched. Someone had come briskly along the sidewalk across the street and turned into Miss Malone's yard. We heard a knock. The door opened, limning a man's figure against the light inside. He entered and the door closed.

"Can you beat it?" I asked admiringly. "She handles 'em in relays."

"The hussy," said Trixie. "I knew she was probably two-timing Hall. I could see it with half an eye."

"I'm going to see what I can see with two eyes," says I cheerfully. "And if I come back blushing, don't blame me. It's all in the night's work."

It was getting late by then. Not much traffic along the street and the people were in off their porches. The shades were down in Miss Malone's house and the house next door was dark. That was a break. I didn't relish the idea of a load of shot from a frightened householder.

The grass muffled my steps and the darkness hid me as I eased up under the side windows. They were inside there all right, for a radio had been turned on, killing anything they might be saying. One window shade was pulled all the way down, but the second one was up far enough to see into the room if one got his face close. I did, wondering who the gentleman was who was following Hall at this time of the evening.

And the next moment I batted my eyes and whistled noiselessly. Standing in the middle of the room, debonair and handsome as he smiled down at the seated girl before him, was Stanley Page, Gleason's brother-in-law!

8

DANGEROUS INFORMATION

IT DIDN'T MAKE sense. I had left Page back at Gleason's flirting with a pretty girl, and here he was using the same brand of ether on Hall's beautiful secretary.

I say beautiful. She was. No wonder Trixie had called her a hussy. I'll bet half the women she met did the same. Miss Malone was curled in a big overstuffed chair like a sleek little kitten. A stunning kitten, with jet black hair, a skin I would have loved to touch, red ripe lips and an adoring smile. She should have been painted; she should have been on Broadway; she rated sables, silks and diamonds instead of that modest smart dress, the humble office job and little bungalow which she had. Miss Malone had everything for success in a big way—and she was wasting it on that big handsome lunk inside.

For I had eyes. Those two were not casual friends. Stanley Page looked, talked to her like she was his own private property. And Miss Malone sat there in the chair worshipping. It was in her eyes, her face, her manner. I grinned as I thought of the explosion we would have if Kitty were there beside me for a moment.

But Kitty was back at her bridge, and the blaring radio drowned out their talk.

I could read lips, but their faces were turned at the wrong angles.

A telephone rang. Miss Malone went to a corner of the room and answered it. She came back flushed, excited. With her back to me, she talked vehemently to Page, gesturing. His face grew serious. He nodded. He said something, and stooped to kiss her. Miss Malone went into the clinch as if that were all she lived for. And I left the window, for the party seemed about to break up.

Trixie said, "Well…."

"Very well!" I grunted as I stepped around to the other side of the car. "The boy friend is Stanley Page." And I sketched quickly what I had seen.

Trixie sniffed scornfully. "I knew she was capable of that. Page is a lady killer. He's been turning the personality on for me."

"He has, eh?" says I, all hot and bothered for no reason I could put my finger on. "I like his nerve! And him a married man!"

"I like his line," Trixie cooed. "He has flash, Ape. He knows his women."

"He's a big four flusher!" I gave her sourly.

I had liked Stanley Page up until now. But the thought of Trixie cuddling up to that manly chest as Miss Malone had just done gave me a bad moment. "I feel sorry for Miss Malone," I said. "Poor kid, he's got her hypnotized."

Trixie gave me the bird. "What you don't know about women would fill the encyclopedia, Mike Harris. That little cat can take care of herself."

"Page is doing very well, thank you," says I—and across

the street the front door opened and Page came out and went briskly along the sidewalk.

"I'm going to tail him," I said under my breath to Trixie. "Tag us. I may need the car."

Page walked straight home. I felt a bit foolish as I saw him enter the Gleason grounds. I was looking for intrigue and I found a man who stepped out between rounds for a little extra battling.

"Wonder if Gleason's at the factory," I said when I joined Trixie at the car. "Let's go see."

The ivy covered buildings beside the big flying field were dark and silent now, with only the scattered night lights shedding a dim glow through an occasional window. We had hardly stopped in front when the watchman was out to look us over. His name was Rucker, and he was a stocky powerful young man with tight lips, keen eyes, a cordial manner when he found out who I was, and little to say. A good man by his looks.

"Everything is quiet tonight," Rucker told me. "Mr. Gleason is over at the hangar looking at the wreck of that plane which crashed this afternoon."

"Alone?"

"Yes," said Rucker.

I went to the hangar, leaving Trixie in the car. The doors were closed, the electric lights on inside, and Gleason and a companion, flashlights in hand, were studying a heap of burnt, blackened, twisted wreckage that had been dragged inside.

THE STRANGER WAS in his middle thirties, medium size, with thinning hair on top, and a brief, alert manner. Gleason introduced him as Rogers, the chief test pilot. Rogers was cordial enough, but after shaking hands he went back to his scrutiny of the wreckage.

"Discover anything?" I asked.

"Enough to make it look queerer than ever," Gleason said. "The place where the wing snapped off is bent and twisted, as if driven apart by a terrific, explosive force, localized in that one spot. A gasoline explosion would hardly do that."

I went off at a tangent. "Are you sure you can trust Hall, your manager?" I asked again.

"I am certain of it," Gleason said just as emphatically as he had before. He eyed me searchingly. "Why do you ask that?"

"Just wondering," I parried. "And what are you doing to make certain the same thing doesn't happen to your big transport?"

"The night watchman has strict orders to keep an eye on it at night. The workmen are there during the day, and I have asked Hall to have a man keep an eye on it also. Are you making any progress?" Gleason asked anxiously. He still looked bad.

I gave him the old song and dance. "Can't do everything in a few hours. Tomorrow's another day. Going home now?"

"No. Rogers and I will be here another hour or so."

So I took Trixie home and then returned to the house.

They were still playing bridge. Kitty got up and scolded me good-naturedly in her fussy, shrill voice. "You disappointed us this evening, Mr. Wormley-Squires, by the way you vanished."

"I am desolated, my dear lady," I gave her in my best

over-the-seas manner. "But the night was warmish and the trip strenuous, so I went out for a drive about your charming town in your brother's car."

Stanley Page was at the table beside us, where the players were, smiling at my little lecture. He grinned lazily. "Don't be too hard on him, Kit. I went out for a bit of a stroll along the beach myself, you know. Have a good time?" he asked me.

"Ripping," I said enthusiastically.

"And you?"

"Not bad. The beach is gorgeous on a night like this." But there was a look back in his eyes that told me he was thinking of something beside the beach. And Kitty had acid under the loving smile she gave him. She did not, I judged, take kindly to her husband's perambulations after dark.

Kitty insisted I play a rubber at her table, and when that was over the party broke up. Gleason returned, and I got off to my room and the sleep I needed badly. It had been a strenuous day.

The next day was easier. I went through the factory with Gleason and inspected his new transport job. It was a corker with a middle placed wing, two motors, a long luxurious cabin, and lines that fairly screamed speed and dash. A full crew of workers were swarming over it. Gleason told me it would be done a day earlier. He added that the master plans were now in the factory safe, away from itching fingers. The local police were prowling around the factory, asking questions, looking wise. From Gleason I learned that every worker in the fabric room had been questioned. One of them claimed the knife. It had been stolen from his work bench a few days before. He was a grizzle-headed employee, with a large growing family, a strict church member, with honesty written all over his face. He was badly worried by the attention he was receiving.

I said to Gleason: "He's all right."

And Gleason agreed, "I think so. They leave such tools lying around. Anyone walking through could have picked up the knife, slipped it in a pocket, with no one the wiser."

Hall waylaid me and took me into his office. His greeter's smile was out in full force, and his bald head and dignified glasses made me wonder how he got that way with Miss Malone. She was in his office, the same stunning girl I had seen with Page the evening before. Beautiful, innocent, alluring.

Her soft hand clung to mine when Hall introduced us. She gave me a twenty-two carat look from deep, dark eyes.

"England has always fascinated me, Mr. Wormley-Squires," she confessed. "Some day I hope to go there."

So I laid on the sugar. "And I hope I shall be on the dock to welcome you, Miss Malone."

"So do I," she dimpled—and I wondered if this was the same dame who had gone riding with Hall the evening before, and then clinched with Stanley Page directly after. I couldn't untangle the answer. Who loved whom, and who was making a sucker out of who was a mystery.

BUT THE FACT remained that Hall had welcomed me the day before as if he had something up his sleeve—and a few moments later the office boy had been spying outside the door where I was talking to Trixie. That was no accident. I wondered what Hall had said to Miss Malone to make her send that boy so quickly. Had she known Hall was after information? Her manner gave no indication of it.

The telephone rang. Hall had to leave the office for a few minutes. I chatted with Miss Malone—and the door opened and Trixie walked in with a sheaf of papers.

"For Mr. Hall," she said, and you could have chipped ice out of the air.

"I'll give them to Mr. Hall, dear," Miss Malone trilled.

Trixie gave me a scornful look as she turned back to the door. It said plainly: *"You, too."*

Hall returned and I went my way, to Sam Davis, the young test pilot. I found him tuning a motor on a test block. Davis lifted an oily hand and smiled at me. We were alone. After a few casual words, I said to him:

"Yesterday it seemed to me you had something on your mind when Mr. Gleason asked you for your ideas about accidents. It did not look like an accident to me."

Davis gave me a sharp look. "It didn't?" he said noncommittally.

"No. Just between us, what do you think?"

Davis slowly rubbed his oily palm against the side of his leg. His eyes wandered over my shoulder into space, as if seeing something beyond the small cement-floored room where we stood. His lips pressed together tightly. I knew the signs. He was not going to say what was in his mind.

"I have no idea," he said deliberately, and his eyes dropped and met mine evenly.

"I think you have, Davis. The police might be interested in that. They have ways of persuading you to talk."

Davis frowned with a tinge of hostility. "Why so interested in this?"

"Mr. Gleason is my friend. His interests concern me closely. I feel I must do all I can to help him, old chap."

Davis studied me for a second impassively and then picked up a wrench and turned to the motor. "I don't think Mr. Gleason would want to hear anything I might say. Take my advice and forget about it."

"Then you know something?"

The boy's face reddened, with emotion or anger. "I don't know anything," he insisted flatly. "I haven't anything to say. You're wasting your time."

And I was. Nothing short of a stiff questioning, with the law behind me, would get anything out of Davis. And I couldn't turn to the law and the local police just now.

"Sorry, old man," I smiled. "Forget it."

The factory was quiet, busy, and ominous.

You sensed it, felt it. Somewhere among all those workers was a killer, rubbing shoulders with his fellow men, speaking to them, passing so casually he could steal a knife out of a busy workroom and not be noticed, and later murder with it, and never be spotted as a stranger acting queerly.

His motive was a mystery, his identity more so. I found no one I could connect with the two who had waylaid me the night before. Hall, perhaps? I asked myself that, and got nowhere. You couldn't damn a man because he greeted you warmly, because he had fallen for his secretary. And that plump baldheaded fellow did not look like a killer. His eyes weren't cold enough. Perhaps Hall knew who it was, perhaps he had a hand in it behind the scenes. But the future would have to answer that. One thing certain, the workers were frightened out of their efficiency. Their placid world had been upheaved about them. No man knew when he would be the next to get a knife in his throat or back. Not a nice feeling. I had been there often enough myself. So that day passed, and the next, and the next....

9

LEFT TO DIE

PEACE SEEMED TO have fallen on the Gleason factory for good. No more violence, trouble. Gleason said to me the fourth morning at the breakfast table: "Rogers is going to take the new ship up this afternoon. I'm going with him."

Kitty objected shrilly: "Wilbur, you will do nothing of the sort! Remember what happened to the last plane that went up for a test!"

Stanley Page looked up from his grapefruit. "That was an exception," he pointed out cheerfully. "Even then the man was saved. Wilbur has been flying a good many years and he's still with us."

"Keep out of this, Stanley," Kitty said frigidly, not trying to hide her feelings before me.

It mystified me a little. Page had been behaving himself. No more night walks along the beach. Even Trixie admitted he was not bringing his personality into her office. Hall, who went riding with Miss Malone every evening, seemed to have the inside track. I caught a look of venom on Page's face a moment later when he glanced at his wife. It mystified me still more. To the public they were a loving married couple, but I would have been willing to bet a sable coat against a broken water glass they hated each other's insides. Had I been a regulation guest it might have made me uncomfortable.

Gleason said flatly he was going up. His sister's protests did no good. That afternoon I watched him take the dual controls beside Rogers in the cockpit of the new plane and roar into the air.

An hour later they were on the ground again. A broad smile of satisfaction lighted Gleason's face as he stood with Hall, Page and myself watching the ship being wheeled back into the hangar.

"It was perfect," Gleason said to us. "A far higher cruising and far lower landing speed than any ship of comparable size today. Its climb is remarkable. The Gleason troubles seem to be over."

And seeing him so cheerful after the days of black worry I had not the heart to say I doubted it. I did say, before the others:

"I suggest, old chap, you have that plane guarded closely."

Gleason grinned agreement. "Rogers will sleep in her cabin tonight. I'm assigning a second man to stay up around the hangar. That will make three, including the night watchman, with orders to let no one approach. They'll shoot if necessary, and get explanations later."

"That should be sufficient," Page commented jovially. "Glad I must run into Chicago overnight. I won't be within range if they start potting."

"Not going to be with us tonight," says I innocently.

"Sorry," Page smiled. "Have to see my lawyer the first thing in the morning, so I'm going to drive in to a hotel tonight and be fresh and chipper tomorrow."

"I might have a brainstorm and go in with you, old man. I'd like to see the city."

Page clapped me on the shoulder and chuckled. "I'll be busy and the whole trip would be a bore. We'll make a day of it shortly and do the thing right, eh?"

"Great."

He didn't want me along. I decided to keep an eye on Miss Malone that evening and see whether she left town also. But a telephone call spoiled that just after we left the dinner table, and Page went up to pack before the guests for the evening arrived.

"That you, Ape?" Trixie's voice came sharply through the receiver. "Listen—I think someone is watching me. A car followed me home from work, and a man has been tagging me ever since I walked out a little while ago."

"Where are you now?"

"In the bay-front drug store down by the pleasure pier. I think he's outside."

"What's he look like?"

"Hasn't been close enough to see his face."

"Go home," I said. "I'll be waiting for you outside and pick him up."

It was dark when I parked Gleason's roadster around the corner from Trixie's apartment house and took up a position across the street from the entrance. It was another great summer evening. Lighted windows were open, people were on their porches, cars and pedestrians were frequent. Trixie came swinging along in a few minutes and entered the building without looking around to see where I was.

NO ONE WAS following her in a car or afoot. It wasn't like Trixie to go wrong on a thing like this. Puzzled, I went to her door and knocked. She did not answer. The door was unlocked so I walked in.

The lights of the small shoddy apartment were turned on. "It's Mike," I called, stepping into the living room, and the next instant I dodged as a dark figure lunged from beside the doorway. He carried a gun, was on me before I could get at the automatic under my arm. He had me cold, and up went my arms.

"So it's Mike, is it?" he snarled, grabbing under my arm and taking my gun. "Glad to see you, Mike. Go in the bedroom there!" I staggered as he shoved me.

The voice was familiar. The build was familiar. And they had already got to Trixie. I cursed silently for letting her come in alone.

The bedroom door opened. A second masked figure stepped back to let me in. He was short, dapper. One look at his fancy black and white shoes and I knew who he was.

"So it's him!" said Harry viciously. "I figured she was buzzin' him from that drug store. And he walked right in, the dirty rat!" Harry swung a fist into my face without warning.

"I been saving that for you, you lousy dick!"

Warm, salty blood gushed in my mouth as my lip pulped against my teeth. "I'll write your name on that," says I, "and mail it back to you."

His eyes glittered above the white handkerchief tied over his face. Yes, Harry was a killer. "You won't mail nothing, smart guy, if you don't button your lip!" he snarled. "Put it on the bed there!"

Trixie lay on the bed, bound, gagged, disheveled. She

had evidently given them a run for their money. An angry bruise stood out on her left cheek.

Rage left me weak as I met Trixie's steady gaze. I wanted to mix with them. Common sense stopped me. I sat on the bed, lowered my hands slowly to my knees. "What do you two yeggs want?" I asked them.

"He asks us what we want!" Harry mimicked. "*You,* you ham dick! An' this pretty little trick who's working with you! Wise guy, ain't you, blowing into town like a Limey?"

"I've seen wiser," says I. "How did you spot me? Gleason talk?" No use playing dumb. And I wanted the leak. I'd have my man spotted then.

"You weren't on the passenger list of the ship you came on," Harry sneered. "We were wise you was a dick before you hit town."

" 'We'?" says I. "Who?"

"Shut up!" Harry's companion rasped. "Don't gander an' try to pump us. You won't cash in on it. We oughta knock you both off and call it a night."

I held my tongue, thinking of Trixie, so little, so helpless.

The idea appealed to Harry. He pulled a thirty-two off his hip, eyes glittering. "I'll lay him out, Joe," he offered.

"Nix!" Joe snapped. "Get that cord out!"

They had strong, thin, silken cord. They hauled me down on the floor, kicked me over, trussed me like a chicken heading for market. The silk cord bit deep into ankles, knees, and elbows and wrists behind me. They hauled my ankles back and hogtied them to my wrists. Harry wadded one of Trixie's handkerchiefs, jammed it in my mouth, tied it in with turns of thin cord. And before he straightened up he smacked me in the face again.

"That's for luck," he said nastily. "An' if we had more time, I'd stay here and show this cutie of yours a good time."

He leaned over the bed and grabbed at Trixie. She kicked him reeling. He jumped back and slapped her face. "I'll tame you, you little cat!" he spat through his mask.

Joe said impatiently: "Hurry up! We've got work to do!"

They finished tying Trixie like they had me. Harry gave me another kick for good measure. "Sweet dreams, copper," he said—and they left the apartment, locking the door.

I lay wondering why they hadn't killed us. Double murder was too raw I suppose. The bed creaked; Trixie groaned behind her gag. The windows were down, the shades drawn. They had neglected to snap off the light. It was welcome.

I tried to work loose. The tight drawn cords only pulled tighter. Cramped muscles began to hurt. My heart went out to Trixie, tied the same way. The tight cords cut off circulation. Numbness began to crawl over me, dampening the pain.

On the bed Trixie groaned softly. My fear for her set me swearing behind the gag. We might both be dead from exhaustion before we were found.

A large fern jar on a pedestal by the window caught my eye. Like a worm I began to inch toward it across the room. Dripping with perspiration I made it. With my shoulder I shoved the pedestal over. Pottery and dirt crashed and scattered over the floor.

TRIXIE HAD RAISED her head to watch. I jerked my head for her to come over. Trixie worked to the edge of the bed, let her wiry little body fall recklessly to the floor, and wormed over. I managed to get numbing fingers about a fragment of broken pottery. Back to Trixie's back I sawed painfully with that sharp broken pottery edge.

The cords about Trixie's ankles broke, she straightened out; and with a measure of freedom in her wrists Trixie worked the cords back and forth over the crude knife. It worked again. A few minutes later we were both free, collapsed on the edge of the bed, trying to rub life into numb muscles.

"That was a close one," I wrenched out.

"The swine!" Trixie panted. "I hope I meet them with a gun!"

Trixie's cheek was still red where she had been slapped. The marks of gag cords were plain at the corners of her mouth. Dried blood was stiff about my lips. It hurt to speak.

"Tonight's the payoff," I said. "I'll call Gleason."

Still shot with needle-like stabs of pain, I lurched into the next room and telephoned Gleason's house. Kitty answered. "Wilbur has gone out," she said petulantly. "Where are you, Mr. Wormley-Squires?"

"I've just come out of a young lady's bedroom," I gave her. "Where is Wilbur?"

She gasped over the wire. "Sorry we don't have the sort of company that appeals to you," she said frigidly. "I don't know where Wilbur is and Stanley has left for Chicago."

"Thanks," I gave her. "Bid four aces for me, sister," and I hung up, feeling better. Mike Harris was in the saddle again, action in his teeth, and be damned to Kitty Page and her social schedule.

Trixie was on her feet, walking about the bedroom, swinging her arms when I returned.

"Lock yourself inside and call it a night," I ordered. "I'm going to be busy."

Trixie put her little hands on her little hips and looked up at me with flashing eyes. "Don't think you're going to leave me behind, Mike Harris!" she snapped.

"Exactly that, madame," said I firmly. "No skirts tagging at my heels tonight. You've made enough trouble."

I was stalling, afraid for her. Trixie marched over to a chest of drawers and took two small automatics from the lowest one. We always carried an extra one apiece. She handed one to me with a spare clip, snatched up her small hat and pulled it on her head.

"Listen," I protested. "You can't—"

"Don't give me orders, Mike Harris!" Trixie snapped. "If you're going out to get killed I'm going along to see that the body is disposed of properly."

We glared; and I thought Trixie had never been prettier in her anger. My throat went tight for a moment. I knew from past experience I couldn't stop her when she acted like this. It seemed to be our fate always to be facing death together.

"Come on then," I yielded gruffly. "But keep back of me, out of my way."

We hurried to Gleason's car. I drove past Miss Malone's house. It was dark. She was out. And I made for the factory. Trouble would be found there.

I was a block from the factory entrance when I saw a car pull in to the curb and a man leave it hastily. A second person was still in it when I pulled up behind.

"That's Hall's car!" I jerked out to Trixie. "I wonder what he's up to?"

10

A SAFE IS BLOWN

MISS MALONE WAS in Hall's car. She uttered a startled gasp and shrank back when I jerked the door open and looked in at her. The reflected light from the car's head-lights behind showed her pale, wide-eyed, frightened at sight of me. And suddenly I was certain she had thought me out of the way for the evening. It was enough.

"We got away!" I snapped. "Your friends weren't careful enough!"

She reached for the steering wheel. I grabbed her hand away just as it hit the horn button. Certain that I had her right then, I hauled her over to the door by the wrists and moved my face close. "Come on," I grated in my best head-quarters manner. "What's on the ball tonight, sister?"

She swore at me, that beautiful little two-timing dame; swore like a Barbary coast dance hall girl as she fought to get her wrists free. And gulped a deep breath to scream. I clapped my palm over her face. She bit it. So I twisted her wrist until she moaned and went limp.

Behind me Trixie said: "She's got a mouth like a sewer. It should be fumigated."

"Get in here and keep her quiet!" I begged Trixie. "Don't let her get at that horn button or yell."

Trixie came in from the other side, gun in hand. "Put that window up and close the door, Mike," she said briskly. "If she tries any tricks, I'll make a good girl out of her."

I left them there, sure Trixie would handle her. Slipping through the shadows at one side of the drive, I made for the office entrance. Everything was still, quiet, as it had been before at night; and then without warning a dark figure moved out from behind a bush ahead of me. It was Sam Davis, the young pilot, cap pulled low over his face, hands in his pockets. I was at his back before he heard me and wheeled with a startled movement.

"What's the idea, feller?" I demanded under my breath. "Come on, spit it out!"

He stared, bewildered. "You—you seem different," he stammered.

"Who you fronting for?" I countered.

His jaw set in that stubborn way I had seen once before. I didn't argue. "All right, come inside. We'll have this out."

He went without protest. The front door was locked. I had a key. Rucker, the night watchman, wasn't on hand when I opened the door noiselessly. Our steps faded out on the rubber matting of the reception hall as I herded Davis before me into the crosswise office corridor. Davis stopped short, so that I bumped into him. Following his eyes I saw Hall standing over a prone figure on the floor.

It was Rucker, our operative, lying face down, with a trickle of blood running out from under his chest. A revolver was lying on the floor where it had been dropped.

I palmed my automatic. "Put 'em up!" I ordered Hall.

He obeyed jerkily. He was glassy eyed, pale; his hat had fallen off and his bald spot glistened with perspiration. He looked at me like a man asleep. "He's dead!" he declared hoarsely.

"I've got eyes!" I said through my teeth. "What'd you kill him for?"

I thought Hall was going to collapse when he understood me. "I—I didn't kill him!" he stuttered thickly. "I c-came in here and found him like this. I made sure he was dead, and—and tried to use the telephone in my office, but it won't work. I was going out for the police when you came in!"

"Says you!"

"It's the truth! You've g-got to believe me!" Hall wailed. "I know you're a detective, trying to find out what's wrong around here. But, my God, man, you can't charge an innocent man with murder!"

"CAN'T I? I'VE done worse! How do you know I'm a detective?" I snarled at him. Rucker dead on the floor and that girl out in the car had me thumbs down on Hall.

He gulped. "Miss—Miss Malone told me."

"How did she know?"

"I don't know!"

Sam Davis gripped my arm. "Are you a detective?" he asked feverishly.

"Yeah," says I. "And you're both in deep."

"I think I'd better tell you something!" Davis said feverishly.

"I think you'd better tell me a lot!" I snapped. "What is it?"

"Mr. Hall couldn't have killed this man. I saw him come in a few moments ago. There were no shots. But before he came I thought I heard a shot. It was muffled, and—and nothing else happened, and I wasn't sure...."

I stared at them, wondering if they were working in cahoots, both lying. But I never saw two more honest, earnest faces. "What are you two doing here this evening?" I demanded.

"I was out driving with Miss Malone, and—and stopped to get some papers I had forgotten this evening," Hall said quickly.

Sam Davis hesitated. "I followed someone here," he admitted reluctantly.

And just then Hall's jaw dropped, his eyes lifted in a glassy stare and his arm went into the air. Something behind me had put the fear of death on Hall's face. I jumped aside, whirling; and as I went a soft, dull concussion broke the low-voiced quiet we had maintained in the corridor. I knew that sound. I hurled myself flat against the wall, crouching. Someone had fired a silenced gun!

That move saved my life, for a second shot came, and I felt the burn of the bullet along my side as I faced full around. The door of Gleason's office was standing ajar, half a figure visible in it, pointing a revolver and a long snouty silencer at us.

A third time that soft deceptive impact came against the silence, and I went into action with my automatic. The double blast of two shots shook the hall, thundered through the building. Glass crashed in the door, the figure standing there sprang back and the door slammed. Hall lay down at my feet like a tired child going to bed, staring up at me with a puzzled air, as if he did not understand.

A crimson smear widened swiftly on the white shirt front across his chest.

Standing there with the reek of powder smoke in my face and my ears still ringing, I told the truth. "They got him!"

I'll never know if Hall heard me. His lips moved. Ignoring that door of death at the end of the passage I dropped to a knee and put my head close. "Didn't—kill—watchman...."

Hall mumbled. "Just—found him... lying—there...."

And I knew Hall was speaking the truth. Men so close to death do not lie. I smiled, put a hand on his shoulder. "I know you didn't, old man," I said.

And peace came over Hall's pudgy face, and he smiled in satisfaction and died.

And in that moment a deep, muffled explosion shook the whole building. I knew that sound. A safe door had been blown. I scooped up the revolver lying by Rucker and pushed it into Davis's hand.

"The telephone wires are cut! We can't get help! Someone's just blown a safe in Gleason's office! I'm going in there! Don't come if you're frightened!"

"I'm scared as hell!" Davis admitted shakily. "But I'm with you!"

Hugging the wall, I rushed the end of the hall.

11

A SLEET OF DEATH

THE DOOR OF Gleason's office was locked. I put the muzzle of my automatic against the lock and blew it open with one lucky shot. As if that were the signal someone had been waiting for, a sleet of death burst through the door. The opaque glass splintered, crashed to the floor. The wooden panels beneath erupted little geysers of splinters. Lead sang and tore the length of the hall.

Davis and I crouched taut on opposite sides of the door. The boy's face was pale as a sheet, but the revolver in his hand was steady. He looked at it like a runner on the mark. I shook my head. The soft click of the inner door sounded and I kicked open the door and lunged through.

Trixie's small outer office was dark, but light streaming through the broken door-glass behind me showed it to be empty. The air was thick with powder smoke. The heavy wooden door leading to Gleason's private office stood like a grim barrier. I heard a window roll up and knew they were going out that way. I tried the door and found it bolted from the inside.

"Outside!" I threw at Davis. "They're leaving by the window."

And as we ran through that hall of death and burst

out into the cool dark night, I thought of Trixie in Hall's coupé. Would they get her in their mad escape?

Gleason's office ran from front to back of the building. The front windows were down, curtained. "They've gone out the back!" I said to Davis.

And as I spoke, a deep toned sputtering roar burst on the night, the sound of airplane motors thundering at top speed. It came from the hangar at the edge of the flying field. Davis and I skirted the factory buildings toward the spot.

An amazing sight burst on our eyes as we came out at the edge of the field. The huge metal doors of one hangar had been rolled up. Like a stage the inside was brightly lighted. And rolling out from that vivid cavern in the black night was Gleason's triumph, the new transport ship. The powerful landing lights built into the bottom of the wing drove a silver path of illumination along the ground before it. Twin propellers glittering in a whirling haze, twin motors blasting the night with their deep-toned roar, the great ship trundled away from the lighted hangar across the field. And a man crawled to his hands and knees in the cement floored cavern, staggered upright and lurched out into the open. I recognized Gleason's tall thin figure as I ran forward.

Gleason's face was bloody, he was still weak and staggering when we met. "What is it?" he asked me wildly. "They're taking the ship!"

"They just killed the night watchman, put a bullet in Hall, and blew your safe, Mr. Gleason. Didn't you tell me those master plans were in the safe?"

"I deposited them in the Winstead Bank vault two days ago," Gleason groaned.

"That explains it! They didn't find the plans so they took the ship itself! They're making a getaway in it! How many were there?"

"I don't know. Rogers and I were in the hangar talking and the other man was outside. We thought we heard shots. Rogers ran out. And the next thing I knew a man burst into the hangar with a gun in his hand and a mask over his face. He ordered me to put up my hands and turn my back to him. Unarmed, I obeyed. I think he struck me on the head."

"Whatever he did it was plenty," I said, reaching out a hand to support him. "The telephone wires are cut. It will take some time to get an alarm out. Got a plane we can follow them in?"

"My private ship's in the hangar," Gleason mumbled. "It's a good fifty miles an hour faster at top speed."

"Quick!" I urged.

Gleason's private plane was a low winged, small cabin model, with the pilot cockpit aft. "Are the gas tanks full?" I questioned bruskly.

"Always ready to fly."

A glance out of the hangar showed the big transport turning at the end of the field, pausing. They were making sure the motors were warm before taking the air. "Get in, Davis, and take the controls," I directed.

"I—I feel dizzy!" Davis gasped. "I've got a bullet in my shoulder—losing blood...."

THE PLUCKY YOUNG fellow had been shot and said nothing about it. By the hangar lights I saw his shoulder wet with blood. Eyes burning, face pale, he was making an effort to be normal.

"Give me your gun," I said. "You'll be out on your feet before long. Get to a doctor and have that shoulder fixed. Come on, Gleason, I'll take it into the air."

Gleason let me boost him into the cabin. A last thought turned me back to Davis. "Whom did you follow here?" I asked him.

Davis told me in a low voice. I whistled with sheer amazement, and then said curtly: "Keep it to yourself until I get back."

I had no helmet, goggles or parachute as I slipped into the small cockpit in the fusilage. Davis climbed up with an effort, snapped the lights on and gave me a few swift explanations. The self starter whirled the motor over, it caught instantly; and over the wing I saw the big transport rushing across the field. It took the air as I looked, climbed swiftly, and headed over the factory buildings toward the lake. And I did a reckless stunt, taxiing out of the hangar and sweeping across the field at full throttle without giving the motor time to warm properly.

We might have crashed any instant after the bouncing wheels left the ground; but the night was warm, the motor not too cold to start with, and I had done it before in a pinch. Luck was with us, for as I banked carefully a few moments later and roared back over Winstead, the motor was hitting steadily on all cylinders. And I wondered if the man flying that big transport ahead of us was not addled. For he was flying with his landing and navigation lights still on. The silver streak was bright in the sky out over the lake. He was heading northeast in the general direction of Canada.

I was no expert at night flying by instruments. But I had flown at night without instruments and I caught the trick in a few minutes. The gleaming pleasure pier, the automobile headlights, the lights and bustle of Winstead fell swiftly behind, and the deep, dark waters of the lake sped beneath.

Still far ahead, the big powerful lights of the transport stabbed down to the lake's surface. It was climbing fast. I climbed too, watching the altimeter, artificial horizon, bank and turn indicator, and as the motor warmed and the revolutions crept up, we began to overhaul it fast. The Lake Shore suburbs and the dull smoky red glow over Chicago itself became visible, and as I caught onto the tricks of the plane my confidence increased, I grinned to myself. Canada would be no more healthy for those killers ahead than Winstead.

The moon pushed up over the horizon toward Michigan's shore. A mile behind the big transport I throttled down and let it set the pace. We were above the clouds now, still climbing. It was silhouetted plainly against the increasing moonlight beyond. I was flying without lights and hoped I was invisible. I dropped behind still more to make certain; and before I finished that all the lights of the other plane suddenly went out, running lights, landing lights, and it became a small dark blot in the moonlight.

That blot turned directly into the south; and I turned, too, keeping it in the moonlight, Canada forgotten. Suddenly plain was that ruse of flying toward Canada with all lights on. They would be reported heading that way. Now out of

sight of land, they had changed direction and were slipping off to some rendezvous. We were at eight thousand
feet and going higher swiftly. They wanted, I guess, to get
as high as possible so their motors would be hard to spot
from the lake surface or the shore beyond.

I flew after them.

12

RENDEZVOUS

THE CLOUDS THINNED out below, the moon climbed, grew brighter as I followed that big transport into the south. Chicago, which would have been invisible at the surface from this height, took the form of a far-off fanciful fairyland, glittering with millions of lights. The Neon lighted buildings, the searchlights waving in the air, the whole glittering night fantasy of the great Fair on the lake front was visible. Watching the instrument board, keeping an eye on that dark splotch against the moonlight, with the steady thunder of the motor in my ears, I sat in that small cockpit and wondered what the end of this would be. Wondered where we were heading. Wondered what those teeming thousands along the lake front would think if they knew of the grim death winging through the night sky.

Chicago, with its police and treasure seekers, was not our destination. The Fair grounds, south of Grant Park, dropped back on the westward horizon, vanished behind the stabilizer; and the compass ring bobbed and swung as the course turned more to the east. The lights of Whiting, of East Chicago, of Gary, Indiana, became visible on my right.

We were heading for a spot somewhere between Gary

and Michigan City, Indiana, flying high, high above the black lake surface. And not long after that I suddenly tensed.

We were past the thickly settled area around Gary, Indiana, where steel mills thrust licking tongues of flame at the sky, and work went on night and day. The south shore of the lake, far east of Gary, was a few miles ahead, almost devoid of lights; but down there on that lake shore one light was blinking steadily. Reflected up into the northern sky, invisible from the shore behind, and from the lake surface, it blinked—blinked—blinked....

That was no lake ship, no airway light, no train, no automobile... Only a plane in this part of the sky where we were flying could see that light. I cut the motor, listened—

Above the whining rush of our plane's swift glide, I heard the far deep murmur of twin motors beating their exhaust back at me; and then abruptly they stopped, and the whole thing became clear. That blinking light marked the rendezvous!

Coming in from the north to that desolate stretch of the lake shore below, Gleason's plane was landing with a dead stick.

I was slightly familiar with that country down there. It was the sand dune region of the south lake shore, desolate, sandy, as little occupied as some parts of the Sahara Desert. There the wind ceaselessly rolled sand into great dunes, and cut them down, and built them up, and pushed them further inland. Trees, bushes, vegetation flourished briefly, and was overwhelmed, and later resurrected, dead and gaunt. Dry sand, and a few shifting trucks were all one found in the worst part.

I had cut my motor just in time. It would have been heard otherwise. The big transport was gliding down swiftly. I glided, too, angling off to the west. I had no intention of dropping into the trap sure to be found by that blinking light. There would be other spots on the flat lake shore where I could set down. It was risky, dangerous, but I had to try it.

The moonlight showed feathery lines of surf breaking on a white sand beach that seemed to go back, back, back—the sand dunes, dotted with dark patches of growth, dry, desolate, deserted. A cove lay some two miles west of that blinking light; and as I swept down to it I saw the brief flash of the transport's landing lights as it landed neatly at the water's edge. A few moments later, without lights, I struck the smooth sand hard, bounced high, rolled, stopped.

Gleason emerged from the cabin as I left the cockpit. He stood steady and his voice was clear again. "Great flying, man! I didn't think you'd make it. Where are we?"

Swiftly I outlined where we were and what I thought. "They're down about two miles away. Must have had it all arranged, for there was a light waiting for them. It's up to us. We can't get help here."

"Why d'you suppose they came here?" Gleason asked, puzzled.

"Nearest place they could land without being spotted. Don't know whether they're just making a getaway, going to destroy your ship, or what. Here's a gun. Let's go see."

Gleason strode beside me as we set off swiftly. Dread sharpened his voice. "If they destroy that plane, I'm sunk!"

"Worry won't help it," I told him shortly. I wanted the

plane, but far more I wanted the man who had killed Rucker, who had shot Hall and attempted to murder me. I wanted the man who had knifed that luckless mechanic in the throat and driven a knife deep between the shoulders of that first sturdy old night watchman.

And I wondered as we plodded hurriedly through heavy sand whether we stood a chance of coming out of this alive. We were far from help, outnumbered. Gleason went up many notches in my estimation in those moments. It was my job. He could have left it to others, but never suggested it.

THE LAKE SURF washed rhythmically in at our left. The first line of the dunes rose in a ghostlike wall on our right, with now and then the dried branches of a tree thrusting stark into the moonlight, like the weird stiffened arms of a corpse. The silence was profound.

Each turn of the beach, each dark object that came in sight against the dry sand, might have been a gunman waiting for us. I walked keyed for instant action, automatic in hand.

That nerve racking walk seemed endless. The beach curved before us—and I stopped Gleason suddenly. The white still moonlight shone stark, bright on the ruins of an old wharf built out from the beach. Against the edge of the dunes was the dark bulk of a queer building. We slipped nearer before I saw what it was. The dunes had overwhelmed an old two-story building. Sand had piled up on the long veranda. At the back and beyond, a great dune had blown up higher than the roof. There it lay, half buried, dark, silent, eerie, deserted.

Or was it deserted?

I found a depression running back into the dunes. I led Gleason into it, up the back of that first high rampart of sand. We struggled along the top, behind the crest. Our ankles sank deep and little avalanches fell away and whispered down the slope. We made the crest behind the old ruined building and looked over.

Plain on the beach were the triple marks of landing wheels. Beyond the ruin below us, the wind had failed to pile the sand for a space of some two hundred feet. And out of that slope thrust the roof of a big barn. The wheel tracks led to its front—which had been torn out, I soon learned—and flashes of light were visible in it. As we crept down the sandy slope to the roof of the barn we heard the sound of tools working fast.

Gleason's fingers dug into my arm. "They've got it in there!" he whispered.

Back from the barn a narrow little valley led away from the beach, winding back into the dunes out of sight. Two ruts traversed it.

A voice spoke below us at the front of the building. "Everything all right, Harry?"

"Yeah—not a thing out here. How long's it going to take to get that wing off?"

"Several hours. We're only taking half of it. We'll have the truck in a barn near Woodville before daybreak, and be in the clear then. Keep your eyes peeled. We don't want any trouble now."

"Hell, we're all right now," Harry said scornfully. "They're looking for us in Canada. It'll probably be weeks before anyone wanders along here and looks in that barn."

"I hope so. This'll be a tough rap to face."

"Forget it."

It was my old pal Harry. He walked into view as Gleason and I shrank against the slope of the roof. His black and white shoes showed plain in the moonlight. A cigarette end glowed as he drew deep on it. He stepped where he could see up and down the beach, and looked out over the lake, but never thought to glance up at the slope of the dune and the edge of the roof. And as he returned to the front of the building out of sight, Gleason whispered harshly in my ear:

"They're wrecking it! We've got to stop them!"

"Keep quiet," I husked, and slipped cautiously down the slope until I was standing flat against the front corner of the building. Gleason pressed at my shoulder, tense, silent.

Harry came back, his shoes scuffing softly in the sand. He stopped, loitered, spat. He lit a fresh cigarette and the yellow glare of the match was close. The strident hammer of tools against duraluminum sounded in loud bursts inside. And Harry moved over past the corner of the building with his back to me. One step—and I had my arm around his neck and my gun against his back.

He made a quick sound in his throat as I dragged him back, and then stood still when he felt the muzzle in his back.

"It's the lousy dick," I rasped softly in his ear. "I've brought that sock with your name on it, sweetheart."

13

THE SHOWDOWN

HIS HAND GRABBED for the front of his coat and he uttered a strangled cry in his throat. So I let him have it on the side of his head with my gun barrel. It finished him for the night.

Beyond the torn out front of the barn a big, closed truck and a sedan were standing, and inside almost at arm's reach men were working swiftly.

"Did you kill him?" Gleason whispered as I frisked the body and got a thirty-two revolver.

"I hope so," I replied, and was just wondering what to do next when it was solved for me. Steps came out of the inside and a man loomed up at the corner. "Did you say something, Harry?" he asked.

"You bet!" I said as my palmed automatic slammed at his jaw.

He yelped once and went down faster than his buddy had. But that one yelp of fear was enough. Inside a voice shouted in alarm, the hammering stopped, and the lights went out. A man ran out into the moonlight with a gun in his hand.

"Drop it!" I called.

His gun swung toward the corner where I was standing.

I shot first, twice, and his gun exploded harmlessly in the sand and he staggered forward and went down on his face.

A frightened voice inside yelled: "The cops!"

Two guns opened up at the corner where Gleason and I were standing. The bullets crashed through the rotten boards. I dropped flat on the sand and out of the corner of my eye saw Gleason do the same. He inched up beside me.

I could see part way into the big barn. They had torn out the front all right. The big transport had been run in tail first. I could see the nose, propellers and far side of the wing. Under that wing a dark form moved to the edge of the moonlight, crouching, peering toward me. I shot once, and it sprawled over backwards, and crawled back out of sight, groaning.

The sand walled the barn in on the sides and back. There was no way out but the open front where the moonlight flooded bright and strong. And Gleason and I waited there with our guns ready. They were trapped, and had no idea how many men were outside.

"Throw your rods over here and come out with your hands up!" I called. "We've got a dozen men waiting for you!"

Someone opened up at us again, but the lead went over our backs. Ringing silence fell when the gun was empty.

An angry voice exclaimed: "I came out here to get a wing off this ship, not to get shot up! I'm gonna walk out with my hands up!"

"Try it an' you'll get a slug in the back!" another warned.

"Wait, you fools! I've got an idea!"

Gleason made a sound in his throat as that strident whisper reached us. It was no surprise to me. I waited, too.

They whispered for a moment and then there was movement back in the barn. A voice yelled: "Don't show yourselves, coppers, or you'll get it!"

More movement—and suddenly the starter of one wing motor whirred in rising crescendo; and then the other. The motors caught with a roar. And I cursed under my breath. They were going to try to run the plane out. Either it had not been damaged enough yet to make flying impossible, or they were going to taxi out into the clear. The plane was trembling, the barn shaking, gales of wind blowing out and sand flying as I came to my feet and stepped out into the open.

A gun barked inside, the yellow lick of the shot coming over the edge of the wing. It missed, but a second shot caught me high on the shoulder, spinning me off balance.

I spread my legs, set my teeth and aimed at the pilot's cockpit in the nose. Shooting fast and steady I emptied one gun at that cockpit as the plane moved forward. The whirling propellers, the great wing swept past me, and over the noise of the motors I heard the spat of Gleason's gun beside me.

The roaring exhausts suddenly died away. The plane bumped to a stop. Out of the windows on the other side three dark figures dropped, ran. The plane screened them as I ducked to the fuselage and dropped flat on the sand underneath. They were making for the sedan parked beside the big truck. I sent one on his face with a lucky shot. The other two leaped into the sedan. It started with a jerk, spewed sand from spinning rear wheels as it lurched around and plunged off along the sandy tracks in low gear.

The man I had dropped staggered to his feet, stared after

it, and then turned uncertainly toward me with his hands in the air.

"Don't shoot!" he begged loudly.

"I ain't in on this!"

He wore overalls, was chunky, with a flat stolid face, pale now and working with pain and fear.

"The hell you're not in on this!" I gave him roughly as I frisked him. "If you aren't, who is? Those two who left you to take a murder rap, I suppose?"

"Murder?"

"Yes, murder!"

THAT FINISHED HIM. "I don't know nothing about murder!" he denied wildly. "Three of us were hired to come out here and do a little work."

"Just an ordinary job, eh?" I says sarcastically.

"We knew," he confessed reluctantly, "that it was a little shady, but we got good pay for it and we all needed the money. But nothing was said about murder."

"You'll hear plenty about it before you're through!" I snapped as I helped him back to the plane. I had got him through the hip and he could barely stagger and groan.

"I work for the Mars plane people!" he choked. "I might have known there would be something like this when I was offered two hundred to come out here and keep my mouth shut."

The lights inside the plane flashed on. Gleason's shout came through one of the open windows. "My God! Come here!"

I left my prisoner groaning on the sand and swung into the big luxurious cabin. The door into the cockpit forward was open. And sprawled half through it on the floor was the immaculate and debonair Stanley Page. Only he was no longer debonair. Blood was running from his neck and from his torso.

His face was lined with agony and he was gasping for breath.

Gleason turned a stricken face to me. "I—I don't understand," he faltered. "There—there's some ghastly mistake."

"I doubt it," I said dryly. "Ask him. Sorry I had to shoot you, Page, but you asked for it. Tell Gleason the truth."

Page glared up at me.

"You're responsible for this!" he panted. "I haven't anything to say! Get me to a doctor!"

"You're going to die," I said callously—and it was the truth. He was shot in several places where that storm of lead had ripped through the small cockpit and found him a ready target.

"Get me a doctor!" was all he would say.

"I don't know what to think of it," Gleason faltered. "He and Kitty were about ready for a divorce, but—but *this*..." He shook his head dazedly.

"Miss Malone will tell you," I bluffed, while I dabbed at the wound in my shoulder with a handkerchief. It was through the flesh, bleeding only sluggishly. "She turned state's evidence tonight."

Page's head lifted from the floor. A terrible look came into his eyes. *"She helped you?"* he grated.

"Sure," I grinned. "How did you think I got away, mixed in at the factory and followed you here? It was put up to her cold turkey and she fell. No murder rap for her. You're going to die and she's going free. How does that strike you?"

It worked like a charm. What Page called that beautiful Miss Malone was not nice to hear.

Oaths bubbled from his lips in a torrent. Suddenly all he wanted was revenge.

"She was back of it all!" he cried savagely. "She was planted in the factory! Kitty and I were through and I fell for her. We were going to be married. I told her I'd be out of a job when I was divorced. She told me I could make some easy money and get a good job afterwards. She was spying on us for the Mars people. Control had passed into the hands of Manny Stark, the Chicago beer man. He was branching out into other business, now that beer was about over. The Mars factory wasn't doing so well. He wanted the Gleason factory and patents. He wanted to bankrupt the Gleason factory and get it cheap. And when he got wind of the new Gleason transport he wanted the wing secret of that. It was not patented yet. If he could get a Mars plane on the market with the features of that wing, and claim both factories had been working on it at the same time, the Mars factory would cash in. He wanted drawings and a wing section, and assurance the Gleason plane wouldn't go on the market."

"So you tried to get the drawings and killed the night watchman," I said.

"HE MET ME coming out," Page confessed. " I knew when the drawing I had taken was missed his story would involve me, and there was a lot more to do before I was through at the factory. She—she said we had to make good before we would be taken care of."

"And you took care of that pilot, Art Ahern, and killed

the mechanic when you fixed up the plane Davis was going to test!" I snapped.

Page flashed me a look of hatred. "Prove it," he whispered.

I said to Gleason: "Davis has been watching this man ever since they both inspected the plane that almost killed Davis. Page inspected the spot where the trouble was, and okayed it. Davis suspected him from that moment, but he was afraid to make a charge against the boss's brother-in-law until he knew something more definite. We followed Page to Miss Malone's house tonight, and saw him head toward the factory with a couple of other fellows. Davis was standing outside when the night watchman was shot."

"*She* was back of it!" Page said malevolently. "She brought men to town to work with me! The new plane was a success, and she got orders to clean everything up tonight before it was too late. She said two other men were coming to blow the safe and get the plans that were in it. Another man drove my car into Chicago and registered at a hotel for me. We were to get the plans, and I was to fly the men here in the plane itself. And then I was to be driven to Chicago where I could forget everything until the divorce."

Anger seethed through Page in spite of his fast waning strength.

"She got me into this!" he wrenched out wildly. "She was making a fool of me just like she was that ass, Hall! She can't go free while I—I die! May God strike her dead! And I *loved* her!" A groan of agony broke from Page as he went limp again. His lips moved silently.

Wilbur Gleason turned a stricken face to me. "It's

incredible!" he choked. "I knew Stanley wasn't much good, but I did everything for him. And he tried to ruin me!"

"Beautiful... I loved her... Page mumbled.

"There's your answer," I said to Gleason. "And I've got enough to rivet this case against Manny Stark. He's big game, even if he hasn't figured in this openly. Get your plane here and we'll load the lot of them in and take them to Chicago. Maybe Page will last until we get there, but I doubt it. This big ship isn't badly damaged, and it will be safe here until you can get men back."

Page died before we took off. And as Gleason's plane climbed into the night sky, and I sat in the cabin with the body, and the wounded and groggy prisoners, I was not sorry. He was weak, ruthless, better dead than alive. We had his accomplices. And back there in Winstead Trixie had Miss Malone. The lot of them would go up for murder. And Gleason would pull through, and once more men who flew from the Gleason field would be safe.

MURDER'S MASQUERADE

When Mike Harris Discovered a Dead Body
Under That Bloody Boat Cover He Went
Back to the Costume Ball to Tear the Disguise
from the Face of the Unknown Murderer

1

A POUND OF FLESH

"HELLO, GOOD LOOKING," I cracked. "What gilded Easter egg did you hatch from?"

We were in the Chicago office of the Blaine Agency. She was a new secretary. She looked me up and down, all five feet six, from red hair to fresh shoe shine. Men have been shot for less than the dirty look she gave me.

"You're a fresh one, aren't you?" she frosted me. "What can I do for you?"

I leaned over the railing and pinched out my cigarette in the ash tray on her desk. "You look like a face slapper to me, so I won't tell you," I grinned. "Is the boss in?"

"Mr. Riddle is busy!" she snapped.

"How sad, how sad," I mourned. "When he isn't, step in and tell him Mr. Harris is out here."

The temperature went up ten degrees. "Mr. Harris?" she thrilled.

"Exactly."

"Mr. Michael Harris, from the New York office?"

"Mike Harris to you, sister."

She smiled at me.

"Mr. Riddle has been trying to find you. We telephoned

"Hoist 'em!" I said

the hotel and they said you had just checked out. Mr. Riddle is having you paged at the New York trains."

"Such is fame," I sighed. "And that just shows you that even the best dicks go sour. I was down at headquarters chinning with some of the coppers. By the way—slip me the catch. Has my aunt died?"

She batted her eyes.

"Not that I know of, Mr. Harris.

"Mr. Riddle didn't say anything about your aunt."

"Funny if he had," I gave her. "I haven't any aunt. Well, here I am—and what does it get me?"

"I'll tell Mr. Riddle." She popped through the inner door. I heard the murmur of voices—a chair scraping—and she popped back. "Mr. Riddle says for you to come right in, Mr. Harris."

So I walked in.

Riddle always reminded me of the moving picture version of a grade A gangster, back in the days when they

On the oval table was a pile of winking, glittering jewelry

were social material. Riddle was stocky, muscular, and running to jowls. His face had a hard-boiled cast of cynical wisdom. Riddle looked like he would enjoy taking the suspect in the backroom and roughing him until the signed confession lay on the desk. And Riddle's real hobby was raising pansies in a little conservatory back of his Evanston bungalow.

For once Riddle seemed glad to see me as he wrung my hand. "I suppose the boys caught you at the station?" he said expansively.

"The boys couldn't catch cold," I told him. "I was at headquarters. Just dropped in here to say good-bye. Why this paging me at the station?"

Riddle said hastily: "I want you to meet Mr. Miley."

I had ignored the fellow sitting beside Riddle's desk.

Now, six feet of a bony and collegiate style chap unwound from the chair and stood up. A lean, pallid hand wearing a gold seal ring reached languidly for mine. A pair of washed-out blue eyes blinked down at me with the intelligence of a cod on a butcher's counter. And the thin, massaged face, with its cute mustache, went through a contortion.

A delicate, piccolo-pitched voice drawled: "Howdja-do, Mr. Harris?"

The languid hand fell out of mine while I solved that facial contortion. Mr. Miley had smiled at me.

Riddle beamed like a plug-ugly who had just planted the body. "Mr. Miley," he said, "is the—"

"Mr. Horace Miley," the high-pitched voice interrupted firmly. And another remarkable contortion took place as a smile traveled up that lank massaged face from chin to eyes.

Riddle covered a frown with a brave smile. "Of course, ha—ha!" he chortled. "Mr. Miley is—er—the personal secretary of Mrs. Leander B. Witherspoon. And on Mrs. Witherspoon's behalf he has retained the Blaine Agency."

I murmured: "Very wise, Mr. Miley."

Horace—he could never be anything but that to me—smiled again. "I have just been hearing what a remarkable detective you are, Mr. Harris."

Riddle said hastily: "I was saying you were just the man for this job."

I speared Jake Riddle with a cold look.

"Now that's just too bad, Riddle. My ticket is bought and my Pullman reservation made. I'm on my way to New York for the first vacation in years. Sorry. Where's your local organization?"

Riddle rolled his eyes piously.

"Two of the boys are shot up and another one has the flu, Mike. One or two are out of town and the rest are busy. I wired Thompson and just got the reply. Here it is."

Riddle handed me a telegram.

Thompson, the eastern manager of the Blaine Agency, had wired two words:

USE HARRIS

I damned myself for letting the Chicago office know I was in town. Thompson had snatched me away from my vacation a few days before and sent me out to the Gleason Airplane factory, north of Chicago. I had almost been killed, lost my vacation—and now Thompson was up to his old tricks.

"Wonderful man, Thompson," I said through my teeth. "He must come from a long line of slave drivers. What's the bad news?"

Horace bleated: "Bravo! This is a bit of luck! I'm sure you're just the man we need, Mr. Harris."

HORACE SHOULD HAVE been planted among Riddle's flowers and tended carefully. He had that fragile hot-house look. Six inches taller than me, I'd have bet a truck tire against a toy balloon he would have disjointed if I'd socked him in the middle.

"I'll give you the low down," Riddle started—but a pale hand waved him into silence. Horace spoke earnestly.

"It's this way, deah fellow. Mr. Witherspoon, you doubtless know, is a philanthropist and public benefactor of the highest degree."

I knew of Witherspoon. Who didn't? He owned one of the biggest department stores in Chicago, had made fifty or sixty millions in his long life as a mercantile buccaneer. Now, he was giving it away. He had established the Witherspoon Foundation of Social Research. His outright gifts to hospitals were enormous. He was the angel and patron of movements to help the downtrodden masses.

"I'm familiar with Witherspoon's history," I grunted.

"Haw!" said Horace. "Then you will appreciate Mrs. Witherspoon's anxiety about the Free Milk Ball which is to be given tonight at the Witherspoon mansion on Lake Shore Drive. Doubtless you have read about it in the society columns."

"Sorry. I never read society. It's too far from the sport page."

Horace was shocked. He hooked a pale finger in the breast pocket of his coat, brought up a silk handkerchief and wiped his palms.

"Really, my deah fellow!" he protested. "You should read the society news. How can you know what is happening?"

"A few other things happen," I cracked. "You were speaking about Mrs. Witherspoon and the Milk League Ball...."

"Ah, yes. Of course. Mr. Witherspoon has sponsored the Milk League and Mrs. Witherspoon has kindly given herself to the ball. The tickets are one hundred dollars. The proceeds will be used to buy milk for the kiddies. Only the best people will attend, of course. It will be *most* exclusive."

"At a hundred a throw, the guests should be as scarce as fur on the stone lions before the art museum."

Horace ignored it. "The ballroom will be filled to capacity. Three hundred and fifty couples have already taken tickets. It is costume, of course. Preparations have been most extensive for weeks."

"I didn't know three hundred and fifty people in Chicago had a hundred dollars."

Horace frowned.

"A diamond set vanity case has been offered by Mrs. Witherspoon for the most elaborate and striking costume. Many jewels will be worn. It struck Mrs. Witherspoon last night that there may be some danger of theft. Er—you follow me? Some chappy getting in among the guests, who will be masked, of course."

"Put it up to the coppers," I said.

"The police have been notified, Mr. Harris. They are sending two detectives to watch the house. However, as an added precaution, Mrs. Witherspoon suggested we engage a reputable detective agency to send someone in costume."

"That's why I wanted you, Mike," Riddle beamed. "This ball is common knowledge all over the country. You know the big time crooks. It's right in your alley."

I threw up my hands. "Okay. Now what?"

"Er—what costume will you wear?" Horace asked me. "Costume?"

"Yes."

"Nix. I'll wear a tuxedo and a domino to hide my face."

"Oh, deah, *no!*" Horace protested. "That wouldn't do at all. Everyone will be costumed; even the servants. The occasion will be a milestone in the social life of Chicago. You must wear a costume. Mrs. Witherspoon will pay for it. Just go to the Mid-Western Costume Company, tell them who you are, and they will attend to it."

"Okay," I sighed.

"Mr. Riddle will have a card of admittance for you this afternoon," Horace told me. "I think that is all." Retrieving a delicate panama from Riddle's desk, he departed.

I said sourly to Riddle: "You've got your pound of flesh. I hope you're satisfied."

Riddle grinned.

"I'd have had to go if you hadn't shown up. Witherspoon is real dough for us. His company retains us by the year. If he wanted a man to go out and sing to his pet goldfish he'd get service with a smile."

"Not from me," I snarled. "And when this thing is over, I'm lamming on the first train. I wouldn't stay if they found you hanging from the fire escape."

As I went out the door, Riddle called cheerfully: "Get a good costume, old man."

I gave the girl in the front office a dirty look and kept going.

2

A DICK IN MONK'S CLOTH

BEFORE LUNCH I gave Mid-Western Costume a tumble. They occupied a three-story building. A chubby young man in spats kowtowed when I mentioned Mrs. Witherspoon's name.

"What costume have you in mind?" he begged.

"What have you?"

He pursed his lips, tapped them with the end of a forefinger, frowned. "I'm sorry," he apologized. "We're a bit short on the better costumes. So many out at this time." But he brightened, rubbed his hands cheerfully. "I think we can suit you. Just step up to the second floor, please."

He bowed me out of the second floor elevator, looked about, called: "Miss Smith—Miss Smith."

Somebody stirred behind a rack of clothes a few paces to our right. A sarcastic voice said: "If it isn't the Ape!"

Spats looked startled, then uncertain as a young woman moved out and regarded us quizzically.

I smothered an oath; "What are you doing here?" I snarled at her.

She blistered me with a smile. "I thought it was one place in town where I wouldn't run across you, Mike Harris."

"Rats!" I snorted. "I'm pushing off *now*." I turned to the elevator.

Spats almost wrung his hands. "Er—if you will step this way, Mr. Harris," he begged wildly, trying to ignore her.

"Let him go if he wants to," she sniffed. "The air will be better in here. He doesn't need a costume anyway. Did you ever see a more natural comic?"

I yelped: "Lay off the smart cracks! I've enough on my mind without you sounding off. I thought you were on your way to New York!"

It was Trixie Meehan, of course; my little pal with her always loving knife out for me. Trixie Meehan, that slender, wistful little piece with the knock-you-down eyes and a face that would panic a movie sheik. Trixie, the best woman operative the Blaine Agency ever had, which was saying a lot.

Trixie put her little hands on her little hips and frosted me with a look. "Your manners are terrible, as usual, Mike. I asked you what you are doing here?"

Spats was mopping his forehead and looking haunted. I think he expected mayhem and murder at any moment. "Uh—uum…" he got out.

"Keep quiet!" I snapped. "Can't I talk to a friend without you having a spasm and a cold sweat?" And I went back to Trixie. "I'm here for a costume. Did you think this was a garage? Run along and do something."

Trixie walked over and slipped an arm through mine.

"I'm getting a costume to wear to the Witherspoon Ball, Mike, dear," she cooed. "Isn't it thrilling? And you're going, too, aren't you? Riddle said he would get you."

"I might have known you were behind it!" I groaned. "I'll

bet a glass dollar you're the disease that tipped Riddle off I was due at the railroad station this morning."

Trixie pouted. "Now, Mike. Is that nice? What if I did say something about the old train? It was a slip of the tongue; and anyway he wanted to hear about you. Riddle likes you, Mike."

"God help me then."

Trixie stepped on my toe deliberately, and sighed. "My conscience is clear. You should know I had no idea I'd be thrown with you. I'll help you pick out your costume, Mike."

I'd have elbowed her away if Spats hadn't been nearing a nervous breakdown. "Scram off to an arsenic cocktail," I begged. "I'll pick out my own costume."

Trixie, glued herself onto my arm.

"I'll see what you're going to wear," she said firmly. "I may have to speak to you at the ball—and, after all, a sense of humor has a limit."

So we went to pick out my costume.

They had all shapes, kinds, sizes. Spats said brightly: "Now here is something nice, in a leopard skin, Mr. Harris. It—uh—would be very effective."

"Lovely!" Trixie exclaimed. "You'd look just too cute with nothing but a leopard skin, Mike. And you growl beautifully."

"Don't," I told Spats ominously, "have another idea like that. My hide goes covered."

Spats dragged out a dozen different ones. They were all bad. Finally, in despair, he produced a monk's habit.

I grabbed it, looked at the cowl, the length. It would

cover me from head to foot. With the cowl up even my face would be hidden.

"You've made a sale," I said to Spats. "Fit it and send it up to my hotel this afternoon."

"The devil a monk would be," Trixie said brightly. "Are we going to lunch together, Mike?"

"We are not. I'm going out and get drunk." I left Trixie there with Spats, who was on the edge of nervous prostration.

But this wasn't my day to get drunk. I taxied to headquarters and looked up Captain Spreckles. We had a swearing acquaintance.

"I hear you're going to have a couple of men at Witherspoon's blowout," I said to Spreckles.

He was chunky, grizzled, gruff as an old bear just out of winter quarters. "What of it?" he growled.

"They've retained the Blaine Agency."

"Huh," Spreckles grunted. "You want us to do your work for you, eh?"

"In your grandmother's powder puff! I want to know what hurdles you coppers are setting up for us to fall over." SPRECKLES GLOWERED DOWN his nose at me, and then chuckled and pushed a button on his desk. To the plainclothes dick who popped his head in the door, Spreckles said:

"Get Kelly, Walsh and Hauptman."

"You must have gotten that last name out of a barrel of kraut," I cracked.

"He's a good man for society stuff," Spreckles replied complacently. "And he's got a camera eye. He can name the rogues' gallery backwards."

"And I can recite Little Orphan Annie. But that doesn't mean anything to the smart crooks floating around. Can he catch 'em?"

Spreckles looked down his nose at me again. "If he can't, you can't, Harris."

"Produce the body."

The boys must have been laying close around headquarters. They filed in one after the other as I finished speaking, Spreckles jerked his head at them.

"There's your hurdles, Harris. Boys, this is Mike Harris, of the Blaine Agency. He's interested in the Witherspoon affair tonight. You might get together. Harris, that's Walsh on the end, Hauptman next to him, and Kelly."

Hauptman caught my eye first. He was a big chunky blond with a Prussian haircut and close cropped beard. I hadn't seen anything like him around a police headquarters in a brace of blue moons. Hauptman might have been a banker or a German scientist. He had the manner, a bit pompous, overbearing, with a million dollar front.

Kelly was a mick, square jawed, blunt nosed, fiery, pugnacious, swaggering. Ten to one his grandfather had carried a hod and smoked a clay pipe. I had Kelly's number at the first look. A wise guy, a hard guy when he could get by with it.

Walsh was the youngest, the nattiest. Not a day past twenty-four, on the Riviera I would have put Walsh down as a diplomat. He wore his clothes that way. He looked like you could peel off a layer and find universities, clubs, and bridge tables underneath.

They stood there eyeing me up and down. Kelly spoke

first. "What do we get together on?" he asked Spreckles with a curl of his lip.

Kelly wrote his own ticket with that crack. He was one of those coppers who get their back hair up when they smell a private agency dick; the kind who think that anything which didn't come out of a copper's uniform is cheese.

"We get together on the Witherspoon Ball," I told Kelly. "You're going masked, I take it. So am I. If our cards run in the same hand we can work better. I always like to coöperate when possible."

"I'll bet!" Kelly sneered. "It's the easiest way to make a reputation."

There would have been a battle if Hauptman hadn't spoken. "Acht, dot is fine. I will be near the door, as an admiral of the German fleet, my friend. Each guest I will see. Undt if any crooked ones show up dot vill be the end of them."

Hauptman rubbed his hands in anticipation and smoothed his close-cropped beard gently.

Spreckles shoved a cigar in his mouth. "Kelly is going as a clown, and Walsh as a courtier of Louis XIV's court," he said.

I grinned.

"Kelly as a clown, eh?"

I didn't say the rest. Kelly got in my eye. He glared.

"Clown is right, smart guy! What have you got on the ball?" he rapped at me.

"I'm going as a monk. I'll be wearing a black habit with a cowl over my head.

"A monk!" Kelly said nastily. "Why don't you take along an organ grinder?"

And so the war was on.

Spreckles frowned and laid down the law to his men, "Harris is a good man. I can vouch for him, boys. If you run into any trouble, work with him. That clear?"

"Very much so," Walsh said crisply.

Kelly merely glowered. Hauptman nodded silently, smoothing his beard.

There wasn't much more to say. They left. After spending a few minutes more with Spreckles I left also.

OVER ON STATE Street I grabbed a quick lunch and then taxied out to the Witherspoon mansion. It was well out from town, on the lake front. Smack in millionaires' row. Witherspoon, one of the first to build out there, had spread himself. In the center of ten acres or so of land, he had built himself a baronial castle.

The main house was rough-hewn stone, with turrets, towers, wings and terraces. A flock of outbuildings were scattered among the trees. There was even a small lagoon, connected by a channel with the lake.

One look through the high iron fence and I decided that Witherspoon believed first in charity at home.

I had wondered why they weren't holding the affair in a ballroom at one of the big hotels. Witherspoon's castle answered that in part. Later that evening when I got a look at Mrs. Witherspoon I knew the rest.

I was a bit dubious as I rode back to town. Spreckles was only sending three men. It would take an army to guard the place properly. Even the watchman I had seen loitering at the main entrance gate, and the knowledge that probably other watchmen were scattered about the grounds, did not entirely put me at ease.

But that was Mrs. Witherspoon.

Riddle called the hotel later in the afternoon. "I thought I'd get a line on your plans," Riddle suggested brightly.

"Then you called the wrong number," I gave him. "How did you find me here? I thought when I checked in this new dump I was out of your reach."

"Miss Meehan told me."

"Where is she?"

"Can't tell you," Riddle says cheerfully. "She phoned in a little while ago and I forgot to ask her."

"You'll forget to wake up some morning, Riddle. What costume is she going to wear?"

"She wouldn't say. It seems to be a secret. I hear you're going as a monk."

"You hear lots of things that are no eight ball of yours," I told Riddle, and hung up, wondering about all the secrecy Trixie Meehan was scattering around. There was a reason for it. Trixie always had a reason. But I couldn't spot it this time. Here we were supposed to work together, and I had no more savvy than an Irishman at a Turnverein tournament.

My costume showed up with a pair of sandals, a rope belt and a wooden rosary. An ornate pass to the Witherspoon folly came over from Riddle's office. I slipped into my costume and almost fainted when I looked in the mirror. What they were doing to Mike Harris in the name of charity was shameful.

I slunk around the room until dark and had dinner sent up on a tray. And when there was no more excuse for hanging around I strapped on my shoulder holster and automatic and made a dash for the elevator.

When the elevator door opened the boy at the controls took one look and his jaw dropped.

"Pull in your eyeballs and drop this rat cage!" I snapped. "This is a party get-up."

He grinned then. "I gotcha, mister. But I sure thought for a minute you was the real thing. That's a swell outfit."

"So is a shroud, but who wants to wear one?"

I went through the lobby like an oyster down an eel's throat, the skirts of the habit flapping around my bare sandaled feet, and half the necks in there out of joint from rubbering at me.

Some fuzzy dame with a skinful of hoopla juice giggled shrilly. "Lookit!" she cried. "Ain't he cute!"

Outside the big doorman gaped.

"Taxi!" I yelled at him, and when the first hack in line jerked to a stop at the curb I dove inside and slammed the door. This was worse than an old maid's first day in a nudist colony.

3

A MAN'S HARSH CRY

I GOT TO Witherspoon's, hot under the collar, and looking for trouble.

We were stopped at the main gate, where a stone sentry's lodge, and a light overhead, made it look like the entrance to a country fair. A guard with a gun strapped around his waist opened the taxi door and shoved a flashlight in.

"Ticket, please," he growled.

"Get that light outa my face before I push a foot in your pan!" I snarled at him.

"Oh, yeah?" he came back nasty. "An' then what?"

He kept the light in my face, eyeing me like I had just walked into a morning lineup. There was enough light outside for me to see him too. He was a gorilla, long on muscle, short on brain space. And he sounded like he was looking for trouble. Witherspoon had picked a sweet set of guards. A second one, no prettier, was loitering back by the gate with a cannon outside his coat also.

I shoved out my pass. The guard looked at it, put the light in my face again. "So you're the dick from the Blaine Agency?" he growled.

"What does it look like?"

"Not much," he grunted; and slammed the door and waved the driver on.

Other cars were following us in; plenty were ahead of us. Witherspoon's big stone castle looked like the prodigal son had arrived. Spangled with lights, doors and windows open, terraces already filling with guests, it was impressive.

I paid the driver, barged up to the front door, feeling at home in my rig for the first time. For on every side were costumes that were no better and some a lot worse.

A footman in knee breeches and powdered wig inspected my card, lifted one eyebrow knowingly and said through his nose: "You will make yourself known to Mrs. Witherspoon, just inside the entrance to the ballroom. She wishes a word with you."

"She can talk to me all evening," I came back. "It's her money that's buying me."

He sniffed, turned to the door and new arrivals. Beyond him stood a tall, chunky figure, stiff and dignified in the uniform of an admiral of the German navy. If I hadn't known what he was going to wear I would have recognized Hauptman by his close-cropped beard and pompous manner.

"How's tricks?" I asked him.

Hauptman spoke past his mask stiffly. "Such costumes! Such jewels!"

"Don't bite the hand that's feeding you," I comforted him. "Remember the kiddies. Where's your pals?"

He jerked his head. "Inside."

I left him scanning the new arrivals and walked through the wide doors into the big room where most of the excitement seemed to be concentrated.

Sweet charity got another jolt when I looked around that vast room, formed by throwing two big rooms together. A florist could have gone south for the winter on the profit off the flowers; and the silks, the satins, the tapestries and whatnot would have bought enough milk to drown all the hungry kids in Cook County.

The room was fitted up as a great Moorish tent pavilion, with a sloping ceiling of heavy tinted silks and sidewalls of silken tapestries and Oriental rugs. The servants wore rich Moorish costumes. Money had been spent with a lavish hand. The Milk League Ball seemed to be given more for the social standing of the Witherspoons than anything else. Thinking that, I barged up to the queen bee herself, holding court just inside the door.

She was dressed as a Moorish queen, loaded with jewels. But the long veil, the heavy swathing silk, the jewels hung all over her could not hide the fact that she was the heavily corseted, dreadnaught type, bulging fore and aft. Through the veil her jaw jutted rock-like.

Beside her was a thin, weedy Moorish Sultan with a fake beard and thick-lensed glasses on his nose. Half a dozen masked guests in various costumes were clustered about them.

"Mrs. Witherspoon?" says I. "I'm Harris, from the Blaine Agency."

The look she handed me put frost on the veil.

"Ah, yes, Harris," she says in a bullfrog baritone.

A TALL, LANKY Moor with a poniard at his hip and a turban on his head stepped forward and whispered in her ear. It was Horace. He could have climbed in a gunnysack and I'd have spotted him.

Mrs. Witherspoon nodded ponderously and turned to me.

"You will keep out of the way of the guests as much as possible, my man," she said coldly.

I gagged on a hot retort and got out: "Is that all?"

"I believe so," she sniffed, and gave me a fat shoulder, explaining to the others: "This man is a detective. We engaged him as a matter of precaution, you know."

"Madam!" I gave her. "No one is supposed to know I'm here tonight. That's the only way I'll be any good to you."

Her jaw came out like a battleship's ram.

"Young man, are you being impertinent?"

"And how could I be to you?" I said through my teeth.

She took it as a compliment. "Miley will show you about," she snapped and gave me her shoulder again.

Horace was floating on excitement and satisfaction.

"*All* the best people are here!" he bleated as we walked off. "Mrs. Ponsonby-Smythe was positive green with envy when she came in. I fancy no one will dispute Mrs. Witherspoon's leadership after tonight."

"Who's this ball being given for?"

"Oh—er—the kiddies, of course," Horace replied absently.

"While they're starving to death, show me around the house. And, by the way, is Miss Meehan from our Agency here yet?"

"I really couldn't say, Mr. Harris. What are her plans?"

"I don't even know what she's wearing."

Horace sighed. "Neither do I," he admitted, with a shade of annoyance. "She refused to give me any information. Mrs. Witherspoon was annoyed when I told her."

I chalked one up for Trixie on that while Horace showed me about the castle. There were more rooms, halls, stairs and places to hide than a rural picnic could find in the Grand Central.

Horace tired of it. "My deah chap," he suggested, "you were engaged to keep an eye on the guests."

"I just wanted to see how the upper crust lives," I told him; and while he was getting over that we went back to the front, and excitement.

The guests were still arriving. Two orchestras were taking turns at playing. I spotted a fancy clown across the room talking to a pretty little shepherdess. Shaking Horace I went over to him.

"My son," I said severely, "I'll bet you're twice as funny out of that grease paint. Get out on the floor, and do your act while I talk of serious things to this innocent young maiden."

She giggled.

From behind the grease paint, Kelly choked: "So it's you! Scram, you redheaded mug, before I take you out and choke you with your lower lip."

"Tut," says I. "And another tut for you. Where's Walsh?"

"Go look for him!"

The girl wasn't Trixie. I left them and wandered to the front entrance, where Hauptman was still stiffly eyeing the new guests.

"Everything all right?" I asked him.

Hauptman grumbled: "These verdammte masks undt costumes! So far I see no crooks."

"Give 'em time," I told him. "The smartest bees don't always get to the honey first. Where's Walsh?"

"Outside. He went out with a young lady a few minutes ago," Hauptman told me.

"Who?"

"A Moorish girl. A little girl. One of the servants, I think."

"So Walsh is at it, too?" I grunted. "I thought you fellows came here to work."

And outside I went, looking for Walsh. We could do better if we had contact with each other.

Walsh and his hired girl were not on the terraces where guests were strolling under soft lantern light. I hardly expected it. Out under the trees where the shadows lay thick would be Walsh's happy hunting ground.

So I went out under the trees.

The lights, the music, the gorgeous gaiety dropped behind me. Automobile headlights were still rolling up the drive from the main gate. But ahead of me, was no dice. Walsh didn't seem to be around.

"Walsh!" I called.

No answer. Here under the big trees it was very quiet. I got the feeling I had cut completely away from the party.

And then it happened off to the left—a man's harsh cry. And silence.

4

BLOOD ON THE BOAT COVER

THE CRY WAS still farther away from the house. It had been sharp with anger, surprise, pain. I was already running toward it. Any excitement on the Witherspoons' property tonight was suspicious.

Wan starlight and a faint glow from a quarter moon lighted the grassy spaces between the trees. And off to the right in one of those grassy spots I saw a slender figure running soundlessly toward the house. Cutting over, I dodged around a bunch of bushes and intercepted it.

A startled gasp, a quick swerve and she would have kept on. I caught her arm, stopped her. She was a small, slender girl in a Moorish costume. Panting, she tried to jerk away.

"Not so fast, sister!" I said, holding her. "What's the hurry?"

"Who are you?" she gasped, peering at me through a heavy veil.

"That would be telling. What are you doing out here?"

"None of your business!" She wrenched out and tried to tear away.

A ring on her finger scraped the back of my hand painfully. In the faint moonlight I saw two glinting points of light. It was a white gold snake ring, with two tiny chip diamonds for eyes. There was just enough moonlight to see the tiny reptilian head against her white finger.

I slapped her hand.

"Be good," I warned, "or I'll turn you over my knee! I heard a man call out over there. What was it?"

She became passive suddenly.

"A man?" she queried nervously.

"A man."

"You must be mistaken," she said.

"Don't give me the run around, girlie. I've got ears. Where's the chap who came out here with you?"

Her wrists tensed in my grip. The veil hid her face effectively, but her voice sounded startled.

"Man? What man? I came out here alone. Please let me go. I *must* get back to the house to work! Mrs. Witherspoon will—will discharge me!"

"You should have thought of that before you took the moonlight cure. You see," I lied cheerfully, "I saw you come out here with him."

"Oh!" She was startled. "Do—do you know him?"

"Now we're getting somewhere, sister. Where did he go?"

She tossed her head.

"I don't know," she said defiantly. "He tried to kiss me and I slapped his face and ran away."

That sounded like sense. "Where did you leave him?"

She was silent for a moment.

"Speak up!" I said roughly. "Want me to take you back there and look for him?"

She answered sullenly: "He was by the lagoon. Now let me go."

I did. She slipped away in the moonlight toward the

house. I turned to look for Walsh, grinning to myself. Getting his face slapped served him right. He should have been in the house attending to business.

"Walsh!" I called as I walked toward the lagoon.

But Walsh did not answer.

A moment later water glinted ahead of me. I came out on the bank of the small lagoon, lying peaceful among the encircling trees. White patches near the opposite bank moved. One of them gabbled harshly. They were the swans, who, during the daytime, moved gracefully over the lagoon's surface. At the far end of the lagoon a small stone boathouse loomed. But of Walsh there was still no sign.

I walked toward the boathouse impatiently. Walsh should have heard me call. He must have heard.

Ahead of me the door of the boathouse opened. A dark figure stepped out.

"That you, Walsh?" I called.

It turned toward me with a startled movement. For a moment it did not answer. Then, moving toward me, it said gruffly: "Who is it?"

That wasn't Walsh's voice.

"I'm looking for a man who was here by the lagoon," I said. "Who are you?"

We met. I made out a gun strapped around his coat. It was one of the guards. He said flatly: "There's no one around here."

"I heard him."

"You are mistaken, mister. One of them swans screeched. You heard that."

"He was here with a girl. She told me she left him here."

The guard was eying me closely. In the moonlight his

face looked square, flat, forbidding. He looked no better than the two at the front gate. Now his head hunched forward. "You saw her?" he clipped out of the corner of his month.

"I did. And if you were around here you saw them both. What are you doing, holding out on me? What's in the boathouse?"

"Boats!" he growled "Don't get hard with me, buddy. Are you the private dick that was comin' here tonight?"

THAT WAS THE last straw. "What d' you know about private dicks? Did someone stand on the roof and yell out the news?" I blurted out.

He grinned. It wasn't a pleasant grin, even in the moonlight.

"The old lady told the boys at the front gate," he said. "I've been in the boathouse having a smoke. If you want to look, come along."

He turned toward the boathouse. On a hunch, I followed. The set-up, looked queer. He had betrayed knowledge of the girl. If he knew about her, he knew about Walsh. The cry I'd heard had not been a swan. It looked as if he was covering up. To be on the safe side, as I followed at his heels, I shoved a hand under my monk's habit and made sure the automatic was loose in the shoulder holster.

He reached the door, threw it open, stood aside and motioned for me to enter.

"See for yourself," he said shrugging. His face had a slight sneer.

"How about a light in there?"

"They ain't working."

"Funny all the rest of the lights around the place are

working," I told him. "There's something sour. I'll follow you in."

He struck from the hip without warning.

I had been on my toes waiting for something to pop. It was in the air. His fist came fast—and I ducked faster. As the blow went over my shoulder, moonlight glinted on aluminum knucks on his fingers. He had been all set to drop me with a smack.

I lunged into him. He gave an explosive grunt as my head butted his middle. He staggered back against the door. I grabbed his legs, heaved hard. He went down, fingers clawing at my shoulder.

His other hand was already going for his gun. I snatched mine out first.

Shooting wasn't in order yet. I rapped the gun barrel along his head. He sagged, groaning; but he wasn't out.

His gun slipped free of the holster.

I knocked it down with my left hand and laid steel on his head again.

This time he rolled over on his side in the doorway and lay still. His fingers were nerveless when I grabbed his gun. But his pulse was steady.

Panting, I got to my feet, struck a match.

Just inside the door I found a light switch. The interior flooded with light from two bulbs.

The guard had lied about that. The inside was not large. At the back was a gas pump, hose, a work bench and tools, several cans of oil. Two narrow slips held two rakish speed launches. The water under them was black, quiet. At the front a pair of sliding doors opened onto the lagoon, which was not big enough to more than let the launches float around. I remembered the canal connecting the lake. Witherspoon had his own private little harbor in his back yard.

Queerly, in that moment, I wondered if he ever took the hungry kiddies out for a joy ride in his expensive boats.

Everything seemed peaceful, innocuous. But the boathouse was a perfect hideaway. It was easy to see why the guard had wanted to get me inside.

I dragged him into the light. He was about thirty-five, and a hard-looking egg. Two to one he had been driving a beer truck in the not too distant past. He was still slumbering. I looked around the boathouse again.

The boats were empty, but the middle cockpit of the one nearest me was covered with a canvas top. Only two sides of it were buckled down. It sagged in the middle, seemed to have been put on hastily. That struck me as queer. It would either have been put on right, or left off. It struck an inharmonious note.

Then a tiny bit of dampness on the gunwale gleamed under the overhead lights.

Gleamed red, fresh! I was at it an instant later, looking close.

It was blood! Fresh blood!

Pulse pounding, I clawed the canvas cover back. I suspected what I was going to find, was prepared for it. But the actual finding was pretty bad at that. Walsh lay crumpled in the bottom of the cockpit—Walsh, the well dressed, likable young fellow, in his gay costumes as a courtier of Louis XIV's court. And one glance told me that for Walsh the party was over.

5

MISSING DEAD MAN

A CUT IN front of Walsh's right ear had bled. Marks on his cheek showed where the knucks had struck. Walsh had not ducked quickly enough.

But that hardly could have killed him. Tugging his body upright in the seat, I examined him closer. He had not been shot or knifed. Then, on the other side of his head, under his curling black hair, I found his skull caved in from a hard blow.

Through the open door, faint music floated from the house. Over there they were laughing, enjoying themselves. There Walsh lay dead. For me the party was over, too. The evening had turned grim. Murder had been done.

No wonder the girl had been running, had been excited, had been reluctant to come back with me. She must have known Walsh was dead.

And, like an idiot, I had let her go.

Then I remembered the snake ring on her finger with its little diamond eyes. By that I could spot her again.

Walsh, in his gay costume, with mask askew on his face, looked macabre as he lolled there in the cockpit. The guard was still out. A coil of light line hung on a nail above the work-bench.

I got it, and in a few minutes had him tied. Turning out the lights, I left, closing the door.

The swans were still huddling across the lagoon. *They* knew death and danger lurked in the boathouse.

A soft breeze rustled the tree branches overhead as I hurried toward the house. The shadows seemed thicker, blacker, and the breeze was like a chill threat. Wavering shadows seemed to reach out ghostly tentacles to obstruct my way.

Fantastic? Perhaps. But I was just coming from cold-blooded murder.

I might have been emerging from a bad dream as I walked over the lighted terraces and entered the big house. About me surged gaiety and lavish enjoyment. These people knew nothing of murder and violence.

Hauptman had left his post inside the door. The manservant was still there.

"Where's the admiral?" I asked him.

He looked down his nose at me, made no reply.

"Are you deaf?" I came back, louder.

He sniffed. "The man went out with you a few minutes ago," he said coldly.

I caught his arm. "Listen—I've got no time to listen to gags from you!" I snarled. "Where is he?"

He jerked away, brushed his sleeve disdainfully.

"You must be drunk!" he said scornfully. "I saw you get the man and walk back in the house with him. I distinctly heard you say Mrs. Witherspoon wanted him."

"For two cents I'd smack you down!" I said heatedly. "You're lying in your teeth. I've been outside."

"I saw you," he insisted stiffly. "I warn you, any unseemly conduct in the house will result in your eviction, my man."

I left him before I committed murder, too. In the ballroom I looked around for Kelly. Murder was his meat to handle:

The big room was packed with dancers. It was a scene of kaleidoscopic beauty. On every side the lights gleamed on costly jewels; more jewels than I had ever seen together at one time; and I'd seen a lot. Pearls, diamonds, rubies, emeralds, necklaces, collars, brooches, rings, bracelets. Half the strong boxes in Chicago must have been emptied to make the display.

It took me several minutes to locate Kelly. He was alone this time, standing in a corner by himself scanning the dancers.

Kelly sneered under his makeup when he saw me. "Still trying to earn your pay check by running around and looking wise?" he asked.

"Shove your tongue in your hip pocket and sit on it," I told him. "Hell has busted loose. Your side-kick, Walsh, is out in the boathouse, dead! He's been murdered. Where's Hauptman?"

"Yeah?" said Kelly. "What is this, a gag?"

"It's the truth! I don't gag about murder. I just left Walsh out in the boathouse, deader than a salt codfish."

KELLY GRINNED AT me. When he answered, his voice was nasty.

"What did you do, kill him? You were probably sleeping off a few drinks and had a nightmare."

"You lunk!" I frothed. "If we weren't in public I'd hand you one! If Spreckles ever gets an earful of how you're stalling when your side-kick is out there dead, he'll throw you off the force so fast your pants will smoke!"

Kelly shrugged, spoke with weary disgust. "Listen, red-head! I don't like you. I didn't like you when I first seen you in Spreckles' office. I never will like you. You get in my hair. You ain't funny. Take your lousy humor out of here! I'm busy!" He glared at me.

I glared back. I think I would have crowned him in another minute if he hadn't added sourly: "I just saw Walsh in here a couple of minutes ago."

"The devil you did!" I exploded. "You couldn't! I left him out at the boathouse, dead!"

"Says you!" Kelly sneered. "He danced past me and waved!"

"It was somebody else!"

"Rats! I came here with Walsh! I know what he looks like!"

Kelly meant what he said.

"Either you're crazy, or I am," I got out weakly. "Walsh is dead, I tell you! You'll be telling me next he was dancing with one of these servant girls dressed in a Moorish rig, with a snake ring on her finger."

"I'm glad you've got some sense finally," Kelly grunted. "So you seen him too, eh?"

"No! Not in here!"

"Then how do you know what the dame looked like he was dancing with?" Kelly rasped. "She was in one of them Moorish costumes. An' I spotted that ring on her finger when they went past. Now don't bother me no more or I'll go out with you and show you what I think of private dicks."

I pushed a hand over my forehead.

"You're crazy!" I groaned. "And I'm crazy! Everything's crazy! Kelly, I think you're telling the truth. I *know* I'm telling the truth. Haven't had a drink tonight. Let's see if we can find Walsh in here. If we can't, come out to the boathouse with me and see what's there. If I'm wrong, I'll take whatever you can hand me."

Kelly sneered: "I'll bite! I'd walk twice as far for a chance to crack you. Walsh is around here somewhere."

But Kelly looked and I looked, and Walsh and the girl were not around. The doorman gave me a dirty look as we went out.

"I never believed in ghosts before," I said to Kelly as we crossed the terraces. "But I'm becoming a convert now."

"Rats!" said Kelly.

"The doorman said Hauptman went out with me. He didn't!"

"Rats!" said Kelly again.

I kept my mouth shut until we got to the boathouse. And then, opening the door, I switched on the light and said: "Take a look."

Kelly crowded through the door, looked around, said: "I'm lookin'! What's the percentage? Where's Walsh? I told you I was goin' to crack you if you got me out here on a gag!"

The middle cockpit of the boat was empty. Walsh was gone. The guard whom I had left on the floor, tied up like a slaughterhouse chicken, was gone also. Both had vanished, absolutely, completely!

6

DEAD TELEPHONE

KELLY TURNED TO me ominously, bunching his fists. "I knew it was a gag!" he said through his teeth.

"And here's where I sock you!"

"Wait!" I yelled as he started for me. "I wasn't handing you the McCoy! Look!"

That saved me. Kelly looked at the blood spot on the gunwale, leaned over, stared at the other spots in the cockpit. "Don't tell me I planted that blood," I yowled.

Kelly's pugnaciousness evaporated.

"It's fresh," he muttered.

"Sure it's fresh!" I came back. "I left Walsh there in the seat, and a guard on the floor tied up. If you're going to listen I'll tell you what happened."

"Shoot," said Kelly.

I told him.

Kelly eyed me intently. Any other time that solemn clown in the quiet boathouse would have been amusing. But not now. Kelly didn't scoff when I finished. Scowling, he said in perplexity:

"I saw Walsh or his ghost on that dance floor. And the twist with him was a ringer for the one you met out on the yard."

I had my automatic out, was warily eying the open door as I said hurriedly: "She headed for the house when she left me. And that don't explain Hauptman. See anyone else in there who looked like me?"

"No," said Kelly.

"Get out your rod. Let's look around here. Walsh's body didn't walk off. If that guard got loose and lugged Walsh away, they're both around here somewhere. I was only gone a few minutes."

Kelly stared down at the black water in which the boats floated. He turned his face to me and jerked a thumb at the water. It was gruesomely suggestive.

I nodded.

"The lagoon would be a good hiding place—for a time," I admitted.

Outside we both stood for a moment eyeing that little placid body of water. Both of us were wondering what the mud on the bottom held. Then we split, searching that end of the grounds. We met at the back without finding anything.

"There's the gate over there, I think," Kelly said.

We found the gate, a small back gate, without a light. A watchman was pacing back and forth before it. He eyed us inquiringly.

"Heard any activity over at the boathouse?" I asked him.

"Nope," he said briefly.

"Anyone come past here in the last fifteen minutes?"

"Nope," he said again. "I've been alone here for a couple of hours."

"A guard was over by the boathouse a few minutes ago."

"You mean Pete Nelson?" he said.

"Maybe. Who's Pete Nelson?"

"An old employee."

"How old?"

"About six months."

"Practically due for a pension," I said. "Kelly, we'd better go to the house."

We cut over turf to the back of the castle. Kelly grabbed my arm and stopped me. "Somebody's sneaking around the corner there!" he breathed in my ear.

The back of the castle was not lighted like the front. The wall loomed up like grim battlements rising from masses of shrubbery. Past the corner of the nearest wing a furtive figure had slipped through a patch of moonlight just before Kelly spoke.

"I'll cut her off in front. You stop her if she tries to run back!" Kelly husked. He dashed off soundlessly over the turf.

A few minutes later brief scuffling was audible. I found Kelly struggling with a slender figure which fought like a little wildcat. Kelly spat an oath of pain as I came up.

"Hold still, you hellcat, or I'll crack you!" he choked.

"Let go!" a muffled, familiar voice panted against Kelly's chest.

"Oh-oh—*ouch!*" Kelly exclaimed, as a heel came down on his foot. "My bunion!"

"Let me look at her," I said, pulling them apart. "That you, Trixie?"

HER VEIL WAS pulled down on her face. She was panting angrily.

"So you finally turned up, Ape?" Trixie panted angrily. "I've been looking for you. What are you two gladiators doing—assaulting women out here in the dark?"

"She kicked me on the shin and damned near ruined my bunion!" Kelly groaned. "Who the devil is she?"

"She's from our agency," I grinned. "We put 'em out like that—hellfire and wildcat. Trixie, what are you doing in that rig?"

For Trixie was a Moorish servant girl also. I couldn't tell her from the girl I had met under the trees. But on her left hand she wore no snake ring.

"I heard how the servants were to be dressed. So I ordered a costume like it and slipped in among them," Trixie said crossly, still making repairs. "No one has spotted me yet. And, Mike," said Trixie hurriedly, "something is wrong in there! The butler has disappeared. The staff is becoming disorganized. And in one of the back halls I met a man dressed like you, walking with a German admiral. He said to me: 'Everything's all right, Mae.' And it wasn't your voice! I put up my hand to adjust my veil, and he said something under his breath and hurried off with the admiral."

"Now we're getting somewhere," I breathed. "What color hair did he have?"

"His cowl was up and he was masked," Trixie said. "I couldn't see."

"Where was he taking the admiral?"

"I don't know."

"If you kept your eyes open you might be some help to me."

Trixie bristled. "There you go, Big Mouth. Your head's puffing already. Stop trying to be a Sherlock Holmes!"

Kelly chuckled; "Tell him, baby. I'm with you."

"Shut up, Funny Face!" Trixie snapped.

"Trixie," I said: "There's a dame in there who's a dead

ringer for you. She's wearing a white gold snake ring. He took you for her. If you could get that ring and lock her up somewhere, and keep your face hidden, you might get an earful. Things are all screwy here. One of the headquarters dicks has been killed. It looks like plenty trouble. Got your gun?"

"I have," Trixie said calmly. She was like that in trouble. Danger never touched her. "I'll slip in from the back," Trixie said. She hurried off.

"What a skirt!" Kelly said admiringly.

"We know where Hauptman went," I said. "It looks bad. We need help from headquarters."

Kelly was a believer now. He beat me to the front porch and in the house.

"Where's the telephone?" I snapped at the doorman.

"In the library," he said sourly. "To your right."

We passed through two doors and found a small room lined with books, empty of guests. Kelly grabbed the telephone. He waited a minute or so with the receiver at his ear and began to jiggle the hook. Then said angrily:

"What the devil's the matter with Central?"

I took the telephone from him, listened. It had that blank, dead feel, without wire noises.

Slamming it back on the cradle, I said briefly: "Dead. No use looking any further. The wires have been cut. We're in for it now. God knows what's due to break loose. Suppose you beat it outside the grounds and find another telephone. Warn the front gate."

"Okay," Kelly said, and hurried out.

I went looking for Mrs. Witherspoon.

7

THE RAT IN THE CELLAR

THE PARTY WAS still steaming up. The music was louder, faster. The lavish, silken, flower-filled pavilion erected inside the huge room was a glittering, flashing scene of animation, shot with the sparkle of jewels. It was filled with the hum of voices, the scrape of feet and the rustle of movement, drenched with cigarette smoke and assorted perfumes. I wondered what they'd think and do if they knew about Walsh.

A moment later I spotted Horace, and walked to his lanky back and grabbed his arm.

Horace jumped, whirled. For an instant I thought he was going to run over me before he got a grip on himself. "You startled me!" he exclaimed with annoyance. "What do you want?"

"Where's Mrs. Witherspoon?"

Horace looked around the room. "I can't say," he confessed in that high pitched drawl that got under my skin. "You're a detective. I suggest you locate her—*haw.*"

"Haw yourself!" I snapped. "What happened to the butler?"

"Eh?"

"The butler!"

"Er—what about the butler?"

"He's gone."

"Gone? I don't follow you, chappie. Where should he be gone?"

"Don't call me *chappie!* I'm asking you."

"Haven't the vaguest," Horace declared cheerfully. "Not the foggiest. And if you'll excuse me, old button, I'll leave you."

I let him go. He would have been a liability. By myself I went streaming around for the hostess. I asked servants. I asked guests.

None of them knew any more about her than I did. Finally I spotted old Witherspoon doing his stuff with a couple of sweet young things who were giggling and wiggling inside cute eighteenth century costumes. The old gander was pinching a cheek and saying fatuously:

"I would know those pretty cheeks anywhere, my dear."

"Park the passion," I said at his shoulder. "Where's Mrs. Witherspoon?"

He cringed, stuck out a wrinkled neck, craned hastily around. You didn't need the dice and a seven to know what Leander Witherspoon's cross was. When he married, he went into the corral for the last roundup.

"Mrs. Witherspoon?" he said nervously. "I—uh—don't know. Ah—you're the man from the detective agency! What do you mean by speaking to me this way, young man?" And he began to bristle and paw for his lost dignity.

"Never mind," I comforted. "People have probably said worse behind your back. I'm looking for your wife."

"I don't know where she is!" he said testily. "I'll have you discharged for this impertinence!"

"You can have the job with a glass razor for a bonus," I assured him. "I don't want it. When did you see your wife last?"

"Er—blast it—I'm not keeping an eye on my wife! Ask the servants. Haven't you eyes? What are you being paid for?" Witherspoon stuck out his chest and glared at me while the two sweet young things giggled.

"Nero," I said, "played sugar daddy while Rome ruined the fire insurance companies. Go on with your act, Mr. Witherspoon. I've got my own grief to coddle."

And I left him spluttering and fuming and searched on for his wife. She had apparently vanished. But I did get an earful as I passed three women. One was speaking in a high-pitched, determined voice. "I can't find Mrs. Ponsonby-Smythe anywhere. She surely didn't go home. The man at the door assured me she had not left."

Pulling in my ear, I went on frowning behind my mask. That was a bit more mystery. They weren't playing hide and seek around the house. The cream of Chicago society hadn't come decked with jewels to hide them away coyly. Horace had spoken of Mrs. Ponsonby-Smythe reverently. She was, I gathered, a social rival of Mrs. Witherspoon. She would be sure to be in the forefront every minute she was in the house.

And a hand touched my arm.

"Beg pardon," a soft voice said in my ear. "Aren't you the detective from the Blaine Agency?"

"I am," I snapped, turning. "What of it?"

It was one of the servants, dressed like a Moor. He topped me by a head, had the shoulders of an axman in a lumber camp. But he was polite enough, mild enough, as he said: "Mrs. Witherspoon wants you."

"Where is she?"

"Down in the wine cellar," he said promptly. "I believe someone has stolen some of the wine."

"You don't tell me. What am I supposed to do—weep?"

That got under his skin. "Mrs. Witherspoon didn't say. But she wants you. She's angry now."

"Take me to her."

Ahead of me, he threaded a way through the crowd to the end of the big room. Pushing aside drapes of silk, he opened a door and led me into a huge dining room. A long table in the center was loaded with food. Other tables along the walls held wine, liquors. Several servants were still putting dishes on the main table. They paid no attention to us.

WE MARCHED THROUGH a side door, down a long hall, and the party faded abruptly. No guests were back here.

"How did you know me?" I asked my guide.

Without looking around, he replied: "Mrs. Witherspoon said you were dressed in a monk's costume. It was easy to find you."

"Seen anyone else dressed like me?"

His head jerked the slightest bit. That was all I wanted to know. "I haven't," he said calmly, shaking his head. "Why?"

"Just wanted to know. Be awkward if someone else was in a monk's habit. Plainclothes men detailed here tonight have orders to work with me. They might get us mixed up."

"You're right," he said noncommittally as he stopped at a door on the right, opened it, started down spiral stone steps. The cellar was deep. The side walls of the passage we entered were stone, the floors brick. Two small light bulbs barely diffused the gloom. The air was cool, damp. It looked, felt more like a dungeon.

"This way," my guide said, turning to the right.

The next instant he stopped as my automatic jabbed against his back.

"Been there before, eh?" I said. "You know what the end of a rod feels like. Don't get restless with those hands."

He stood still. Slowly his head turned, eyeing me over one shoulder. "What's the idea?" he asked. His voice was calm enough.

"I'm left-handed every Thursday," I said. "It gives me a headache to walk to the right. To the left, big boy, to the left. And one yip out of you and I'll open your head like a used sardine tin."

We went left.

I hadn't realized how much ground Witherspoon's house covered until we walked to the end of the passage and turned to the left again. It was almost a second house underground. Ahead of us was another flight of steps leading up. A word from me stopped him beside a door. I tried the knob. It was locked. The next door swung in, however. The room beyond was dark; but enough light struck in from the passage to show stacked trunks.

I herded him in. "Shuck out of that uniform, sucker."

"*What?*" he growled.

"Go on—make it snappy." I tickled him in the ribs with the automatic. "Don't make me lay you on the floor and undress the corpse." I yanked the turban off his head. He had a prison hair cut.

"Hah—a stirbird," I said. "I thought you walked funny. What icebox were you in lately?"

"You're crazy!" he snarled. "Mrs. Witherspoon asked me to get you. You'll get fired for this!"

"I'm all burned up now. What kind of a sap did you think I was? That gag wouldn't fool the kiddies if a gallon of free milk was thrown in. Get out of that Halloween costume quick. This is the last call for volunteers."

He peeled. And when his duds were lying on the floor he didn't look like a high society servant to me. He was young, but hard—mean. And he wore a gun under his arm. I grabbed that.

I threw him my habit. "Get into that and flop down on the floor."

He swore. "Smart copper!" he sneered. "Wait for the kickback on this."

"Yeah—smart," I comforted. "The kickback will make you sick. Down, Rover."

My costume was too small for him; but he got wrapped in it after a fashion and went down on the floor swearing like a deacon who forgot to foreclose. I tied him with the rope belt which had been around my habit, and gagged him with his undershirt. A couple of trunk straps completed the job. Then I slipped into his Moorish rags. They were a little big, but a few tucks here and there made them do. I was even able to use his shoes.

Rolling him over behind the door, I cocked the turban on my head.

"You look like a first class rat," I told him. "So down here with the rats you stay. I hope you aren't moldy when they find you."

He was raging behind the gag when I closed the door.

I went back toward the steps down which we had come, figuring that on beyond them, where he had wanted to take me, might be something interesting. But just before I made the turn in the passage I heard a muted scuffle of sound ahead. A voice wrenched out something that sounded suspiciously like a cry for help. I made that turn on the run.

And I hadn't gone a half dozen steps when a door ahead, beyond the stairs, opened suddenly. A man plunged out, caught his balance, dashed toward the stairs.

Out of the doorway behind him a second figure lurched, steadied on spread legs, and, lifting a gun, fired twice.

8

THE BUTLER DIES

THE CRASHING REVERBERATIONS of the two shots were ringing in my ears as the running man pitched forward and dropped in a heap on the damp bricks. He gasped, writhed, and went still.

I was ready by then to shoot it out myself. That was cold-blooded murder. The victim looked to be about forty-five or -six years old, dressed in black, and somewhat of a husky. And certainly not a gunman, a killer, from the little I had seen in the dim light, Then I got my second surprise.

The killer had seen me without doubt. But he staggered, leaned against the passage wall a moment, and lurched forward, heavy-footed, paying little attention to me. The automatic hung down at his side. He was swearing nastily in a disjointed monotone. Blood was streaming down over one cheek.

And then I remembered that I was wearing another costume. He took me for someone else. Stopping by the figure he stirred it with a foot, then, kicked it viciously.

"'That so-an'-so hammered on the door an' wanted to tell me something!" he said thickly. "When I unlocked it an' went in, he cracked me on the face with a chair. Knocked me down, it did, an' he busted out the door. Figured he could get upstairs before I could stop him." He kicked the limp body again. "But I showed the so-an'-so!" he said. "He ain't swingin' any more chairs. Look at my face bleeding!"

He was another of the Moorish brethren. His turban was awry on his head. He jerked it off, mopped at the blood with it. Inspecting the result, he spoke out of the corner of his mouth. "Did you get that man from the Blaine Agency?"

"Uh—uh," I said.

"Why the devil didn't you?" he jerked out.

"Couldn't find him," I mumbled.

"You better!" he said viciously.

"You killed him," I says, edging close with the gun ready in my hand.

"What of it? He damned near killed me!" A thought struck him. Standing there, bloody turban in one hand and gun in the other, he stared at me. "Say!" he exclaimed. "You don't sound like Bert. You're mighty short, too, all of a sudden!"

His gun was already coming up when I slammed him on the side of the jaw with my automatic. He pulled the trigger as he went down. The bullet cratered the bricks an inch from my foot. But that one shot was all. Gun hanging loose in his fingers, he collapsed in a limp heap on top of the dead man. Both sides of his face were bloody now.

I hauled him off, examined the man in black, the missing butler. He was quite dead. One shot had caught him in the spine, the other had bored through his neck. He was bleeding plenty, but probably had never known what had hit him.

I was shaken when I stood up. Walsh's death had been

bad enough. But I hadn't seen that. In a way it had been detached. This second killing completed a vivid warning of bloody mystery.

It was a cinch the underworld was on the loose up there as it was down here in the cellar where I had been decoyed. Not the petty larceny, second-story underworld. This was a big shot play—big business. Every bit of detail must have been well planned in advance. Someone had known the three headquarters dicks were going to be here tonight. Had known how they were to be dressed. I couldn't see how they had found out. And my heart did a nose-dive and cold sweat almost broke out as I thought of Trixie Meehan.

I had sent Trixie off on a bold play. Trixie would try to go through with it. She didn't know what she was up against; didn't know that death might be the penalty for failure.

Catching the killer by the heels, I dragged him through the doorway from which he had emerged. It was dark beyond, but in he went. The room was stacked with old furniture. He was still out, for I had cracked him hard. A key was in the door, with several others attached to it on a key ring. I locked the door, took the keys and was turning to the steps when muffled speech caught my attention.

Further along the corridor someone was talking in a low, harsh monotone. I went toward the source on my toes. Behind the second door on the left I located the voice. Someone in there was pacing about, swearing lustily. I unlocked the door, stepped inside—and a thunderbolt struck me, knocked me off my feet, carried me to the floor. Fingers dug into my throat. A big hand clapped over my gun, wrenched it aside where I couldn't have shot and hit anything if I'd tried. A furious voice rasped over my face:

"Now I show you!"

His whole weight was pressing his hand in my throat. I couldn't breathe, speak. The dim lights in the passage flickered to rainbow hues as the blood hammered in my head and everything swam before my eyes. I wondered if I was going to be choked unconscious before I could stop him. I let go the automatic, smacked the hard edge of my hand against the straining forearm muscles that were choking me. A grunt of pain, and the arm relaxed, the fingers slid off my throat.

"Hauptman!" I gasped.

"Vat—vat is?" Hauptman straightened up, peering at me in astonishment.

"Get off, you damn fool! I'm Harris, of the Blaine Agency!"

Hauptman slowly rolled off to a wary crouch; got up when I did. "Maybe I made a mistake," he admitted reluctantly.

"Don't make any more of them around me!" I said, fingering my sore throat, "I try to let you out and you try to kill me!"

"You got on a different costume," he grumbled. "You look like one of the swine who put me in here."

HAUPTMAN WAS CONSIDERABLY mussed himself. And mad. Larding his story with lurid oaths, he told how a man dressed in a monk's costume had summoned him to Mrs. Witherspoon. Down in the cellar passage a man dressed in a Moorish costume had drawn a gun and, helped by the monk, had locked him in the dark room where I had found him. He had heard the shots, had been like a caged bear in his inability to do anything.

No one had come down from the upper house to investigate the shots.

"Get yourself together, Hauptman!" I snapped. "Here's a gun. There's trouble upstairs." I told him what I knew.

Hauptman's close-cropped hair fairly bristled as he listened. His pompous manner was gone now. He was a hard-boiled copper when he waved the automatic and ground out:

"We go up undt take them, eh?"

"Wait a minute!" I said, hanging on his arm as he started for the stairs. "Not that way! You'll have a riot. Anyone we want will lam during the excitement. Kelly has gone to telephone headquarters. Any minute now a hundred cops ought to be surrounding the grounds. We've got to hold everything quiet until then. Mrs. Witherspoon and a Mrs. Ponsonby-Smythe are gone. We must locate them. And there's a girl from the Blaine Agency upstairs who doesn't know what she's up against. And there's a man dressed like me, and one rigged up like Walsh whom we want. We've got two locked up down here. But the main thing is to keep everything quiet until headquarters gets here. How about it?"

Hauptman nodded enthusiastically. "Sure!" he agreed. "We will wait—just like that." He half clenched the fingers of one hand for a moment and then snapped them shut, as if engulfing the lot we were after.

"Fit that mask back on your face. We'll go up and look wise."

So we went up together, cut through the big dining room into the ballroom once more. It hadn't changed. You would have thought life was nothing but froth and bubbles. There they were dancing, laughing, talking—and beneath them a man had just been shot to death. It reminded me of the French court before the revolution, dancing to their doom. Among them at this moment were desperate men working to a preconceived plan. And the bait was surely those glittering baubles which hung about white throats.

First I wanted Trixie; and I didn't know where to find her. To Hauptman, I said: "See if you can find the guys dressed like Walsh and me. They're dangerous."

"Watch me!" Hauptman rumbled, and strode off.

Horace was talking to a dowager decked with jewels when I appeared before him. His mask hid his face. But his mouth gaped, went through a marvelous contortion before he spoke. His voice sounded as if it were being squeezed out of taffy.

"Uh—where did you come from? Pardon, dear lady, I must talk with this man." He bowed from well oiled hips and dragged me off by an arm. "Your costume!" he babbled. "What—what's happened to it?"

"I'm a chameleon. I change with the weather."

"Did you find Mrs. Witherspoon?" he questioned hurriedly.

"I didn't." And then I proceeded to break one of my ironclad rules. I told a sap what I knew. "I found the butler. He's dead."

"Dead?" Horace croaked. He stared at me with something close to horror. The information had hit him hard. His tongue came out, moistened his lips. "How do you know he's dead?"

"I saw him shot."

"Where?" Horace bleated. "I say, you're pulling my leg, aren't you?"

"Downstairs, in the basement. Listen, I need your help. Crooks are among the guests and servants in disguise. They're after the jewels, of course. Already they've killed one of the men from headquarters and the butler. No telling what they'll do next."

"You—you can't mean it!" Horace squeaked. "We must get the police, of course! I'll telephone them!"

"Nix," I said. "You're wasting your time. Telephone line is cut, Kelly, from headquarters, has gone outside to telephone. The police will be here quick. Mrs. Witherspoon and Mrs. Ponsonby-Smythe are missing."

Horace groaned: "This is ghastly! I—uh—what have you done so far?"

"Two of the mob are locked up downstairs. They had one of the headquarters men down there, I brought him up. How many of the menservants can you trust?"

"I d-don't know," Horace stuttered. "All of them, I suppose. They were investigated before they were employed. Mrs. Witherspoon is strict."

"Evidently, from the cut-throats on her staff tonight. Now listen! The butler is dead. He can't help me. You'll have to try. Round up the servants who might be of some use. Don't get any crooks among them. Then call me. I'll give them orders. Got it?"

"Y-yes," Horace said feverishly.

"And don't," I said as he started off, "go with anyone who wants you to see Mrs. Witherspoon. It's a stall. You're apt to wind up with a slug in you."

I went looking for Trixie, feeling guilty as I did so. In

the house was a master brain, controlling the crooks. He should be located first. But I had to get Trixie and warn her.

I was halfway through the dining room when a door ahead of me flew open. A Moorish girl with a snake ring on her finger entered hastily. I made for her warily. She passed without giving me a tumble. I grabbed her arm.

"Quiet, sister!" I said. "Let's get off alone and talk."

She had a gun in my ribs before I finished.

"Don't move!" she warned, jerking her arm free. "*You'll* do the walking with *me*."

"Trixie!"

"Mike!"

HER GUN VANISHED as quickly as it had appeared. "What is this, a guessing game?" Trixie asked sarcastically from behind the veil. "I almost put a bullet in you then!"

Two veiled girls were working around the table. They stopped, listening, watching us curiously. I figured they were all right or they wouldn't be working. "Go on with it," I said to them. "This is private business."

The nearest, pert and slender, tossed her head and sniffed behind her veil.

"You'd think everything in this house tonight was private business. Strange people on the staff; the butler gone; Mrs. Witherspoon not around to give orders! She was holding a gun then, wasn't she?"

"It's a water pistol," Trixie explained sweetly. "By the way, where is Mrs. Witherspoon?"

The girl tossed her head again. "How should I know? I'm not paid to watch her. But if she doesn't appear soon and give orders, this ball will wind up in a mess. None of the servants know what to do."

"I'll tell you what to do. Keep your mouth shut and go on with your work."

Trixie joggled my elbow, said sarcastically: "Come out in the hall, loud mouth. Are you trying to play teacher and kindergarten?"

"If I knew how to teach, I'd have taught you better manners long ago," I gave her.

Trixie kicked me on the ankle as we headed for the door.

"There you go!" I grated. "Who am I fighting, you or the crooks?"

So the battle was on.

But we ditched it out in the hall. "I see you've got the ring," I said.

"She's locked up in a linen closet in the servants' wing, Mike. And she's a gun moll. You should have heard her language. It's a wonder she didn't put a bullet in you. None of you men have any sense about women."

"Lay off, lay off," I begged. "I've got enough grief without you jawing under my chin. Take that ring off and forget about it. I just saw the butler knocked off. They've cut the telephone wires, isolated the house. I don't want you sticking out your neck for the ax."

"Sir Galahad, as usual," Trixie sniffed, but her voice was softer. "I was trying to find you and warn you, Mike. Back there a few minutes ago a man dressed in a monk's costume took one look at the ring on my finger and told me to hurry upstairs. He said Riorgen wanted me."

"*Riorgen?*"

"You're not deaf. Riorgen, he said."

And that was the key I needed. Danny Riorgen was one of the most ruthless of the north side big shots. No wonder the crooks seemed well organized. Riorgen would have every detail planned out.

It was the new trend of crime the underworld was taking. With booze and beer rackets shot, the mobs were desperate for money. They were turning to other sources of revenue. What could be sweeter than this house full of priceless jewelry?

And to meet Danny Riorgen's mob, headquarters had only sent three plainclothes men. It was like meeting an elephant's charge with a popgun.

I grabbed Trixie's arm. "You say Riorgen's upstairs?"

"Yes. But you're not going up there after him, Mike."

"No?"

Trixie stamped her foot.

"You idiot! You red-headed numbskull! I know who Danny Riorgen is. He won't be alone up there. If they killed the butler a few minutes ago, what is to stop them from killing *you?*"

"Nothing, sweet—if they kill first. But they won't be looking for me in this costume."

Trixie put her little hands on her little hips and glared at me through her veil. "Mike! Don't you dare go up there!"

"Sure," I kidded her. "Wouldn't think of it. I'm going to grab this guy who looks like me."

"He's gone. I don't know where he went."

Trixie put her hand on my arm. Her voice softened. "Mike, please! You're not a riot squad. They'll blast you if they know who you are."

"But they don't—and they won't, kid," I said, patting her hand.

We were always like that in a pinch. It tied me in knots

to think of anything happening to Trixie. And I guess she would have missed me a little.

"It's no good," I went on. "I'm going up. And you stay back."

She nodded. "Go up the back stairs, Mike. Here—I'll show you."

She guided me back to the stairs. We stopped there a moment, staring at each other.

"Remember," I said gently, "no tagging, Trixie. I can't have you on my mind up there."

She nodded dumbly. And as I started up the stairs she said suddenly: "Oh, Mike—about this Miley person, this secretary of Mrs. Witherspoon's. Why should he run up those stairs as if the devil were at his heels?"

"Did he?"

"Yes. Just before I met you in the dining room."

"Queer," I said. "I'll think it over."

Horace was on my mind as I went up. I had asked him to round up the male servants. That hardly called for frantically dashing upstairs. Then Horace left my mind. The staircase let me into an upper hall. And out of a cross corridor just in front of me dashed my duplicate, the man in the monk's habit!

9

NINE MEN TO LICK

LIFE HAS LITTLE surprises like that. I knew it called for action. He had the same idea. Dodging, he grabbed under his robe.

He was about my size. I knew I could take him. Jumping in close I swung from the hip. Over his guard—*smack*—and he reeled into the wall. A left and a right again to his face jarred me when they landed. It had to be quick, before his rod came out. The last two knocked his head against the wall where he had staggered. He tried to duck. I kneed him in the groin—and suddenly he was on the floor writhing in agony. And still trying to draw a gun.

It was over like that in short seconds—but his mouth was still not closed. Snatching the gun from his hand as he fumbled it out, I dragged him up, choking him.

That finished it. Dazed, he could only gasp, gag.

Dragging him to the nearest door by the neck, I hauled him into a luxurious bedroom. Kicking the door shut gave the privacy I wanted. It was no time for first aid. I threw him on the bed. Pushing the cowl back, the mask off his face, I found a thin, sharp-faced young man with a long nose and a wide, treacherous mouth from the corner of which blood was trickling.

His shifty eyes rolled up at me as I caught his throat in one hand and shoved my gun under his nose with the other.

"All right, Rat!" says I. "The party's over for you. Will you talk?"

He sneered at me and shut his jaw.

I slapped him. It was the only treatment these mobsmen understood. Try to argue, be reasonable, and they'd laugh you out of the picture. They fattened on fear in others.

"You aren't in a station house with a bunch of coppers," I told him. "No smart lawyer's going to spring you and holler about third degree brutalizing. You're a bunch of rats on the loose here tonight. No jury will shed any tears over what happens to you. Come on—how much do I have to give you before you talk?"

His face was the pasty color of dough. He reminded me of a cornered rat whose bright, beady eyes were shifting around for an out. He licked his lips, lay dumb on the bed.

"You asked for it and here it is!" I slapped him on the mouth with the blue steel of my automatic, pulping his lips, breaking teeth.

Brutal? Sure! This wasn't a tea party. He and his pals would do worse if they thought it would help. They'd rub me out with no more mercy than that poor devil had received in the basement.

He cowered on the bed, hands before his face, blood showing between his fingers.

"Don't," I said, "make me tear your face off."

He couldn't take it. His kind were all yellow away from guns and protection. "My God, don't!" he spewed through broken lips. "I'll talk!" His eyes followed my automatic in horrified fascination as I lowered it.

"Where's Riorgen?" I said.

He stiffened in surprise, rolled shifty eyes up at me. The question had caught him off guard. His mind was readable. Afraid of me—he was more afraid of Danny Riorgen. I might break his face. Riorgen would kill him.

"Don't know," he mumbled.

By the hair I forced his head back, raised the automatic again. "Giving me the run around, eh?"

"Don't! Riorgen's in the house here!"

"Where?"

"Downstairs," he wrenched out.

I dropped the gun across his nose. Sure I was a beast. I was gambling with death. If Danny Riorgen escaped tonight others would die before the cops got him cold again. And if I blundered around looking for Riorgen I'd probably collect bullets before I found him. This writhing, groaning, treacherous little rat on the bed was the only sure card I had to play. And he had probably earned the electric chair a dozen times.

That last broke his spirit. Ever see a man with the fear of God in his rotten soul? It's not a pretty sight. I wasn't proud of myself.

He crawled. He groveled. He pleaded brokenly, incoherently. "I'll tell you!" he wept. "Riorgen's upstairs here. Along that hall, to the left at the first turn. The second door on the right."

"How many men are with him?"

"Two."

"What's he doing there?"

"Collecting from the guests."

"How many men has he got?"

"We brought fourteen—an' the drivers of the cars," he mumbled.

Fourteen!

I THINK I went weak for a moment then. What chance did Trixie, Hauptman and I have against the nine who were left?

"Where are the others?"

"Around," he whispered—and fainted there on the bed.

But his pulse was strong. The pain, the loss of a little blood wouldn't hurt him. Ripping a sheet into strips, I tied, gagged him; and dumped him in a clothes closet.

Picking his gun off the hall floor, I started for Danny Riorgen. Nine men left. Riorgen and two others ahead; six more around. I made the turn, stopped before the second door on the right. It was closed, but someone was talking inside.

I paused, drew a deep breath. About all I could do was hold them until the coppers arrived. Any instant I expected to hear the shrill of police sirens, the sudden tumult of the law about the house. And Danny Riorgen must not blast his way out to safety. I opened the door, jumped through into the room beyond.

It was a sitting room, furnished with period pieces, inch thick rugs. Brightly lighted, quiet, peaceful. Three men were standing about an oval table in the center of the room. They turned quickly as I came in.

"*Hoist 'em!*" I said.

Hands went up. Shoving the door back with a heel I moved toward them slowly. One was dressed as a swaggering pirate, one was another Moorish manservant. And the third, beyond the table, facing me, was another Walsh, in a Louis XIV court costume.

On the oval table, winking, glittering, under an overhead light, was a pile of jewelry which widened my eyes. Diamond and pearl necklaces, diamond bracelets, emerald brooches, bloodred rubies rich and costly. The whole stock of some big jewelry stores wouldn't buy that pile.

"Which one of you is Danny Riorgen?" I asked.

No one answered.

But I knew. The Moor was out. The pirate was too short, stocky to fit pictures I had seen of Danny Riorgen. The slender duplicate of Walsh was Riorgen. And I had a flash of admiration for his nerve, coolly dancing down there among the guests and waving at Kelly, while he scanned the jewelry.

Riorgen spoke, softly, politely. "What is this? A little surprise?"

"A big one, Riorgen," I told him.

"So you know me, copper? You're too smart for the Blaine Agency."

"Never mind the soap. All three of you line up to the wall. And don't go for your rods."

Riorgen laughed. He didn't seem worried. "Why should we?" he said. "Line up, boys. He won't cut us down from behind."

They faced the wall, hands up. It was too easy. Something was wrong. With a shock of surprise I recalled that Riorgen knew I was from the Blaine Agency. He had picked me out under my new costume.

As I collected the guns they all carried I asked: "How do you know I'm from the Blaine Agency, Riorgen?"

He laughed without turning his head. "I can always spot a sucker."

Which meant nothing. But he had something up his sleeve. "This will mean the hot seat for all of you," I said.

Riorgen laughed again.

"Yeah, Copper? Who put such ideas in your head?"

And before I could answer, someone opened the door. I dropped two guns on the floor, shoved one that way, figuring it was one of Riorgen's mob. And then grinned with relief when Horace busted in, saw the little scene and stopped abruptly.

"Er—what's this?" Horace gasped. "Ah—put that gun away, chappie. I'm afraid of them."

"I never thought I'd be so glad to see you," I told him. "Come over here and give me a hand."

Horace sidled over nervously. "I—uh—don't understand," he said. "Who are these men? You're not—uh—holding up our guests?"

"I'm not! Grab a gun and help me. This is Danny Riorgen and a couple of his men. Look on the table."

Horace stooped and gingerly lifted one of the guns I had dropped. "Dear me," he squeaked. "I—uh—am trembling. I don't know what to do."

And with that he cracks me across the wrist with the gun and grabs the automatic out of my numb hand.

10

ON THE SPOT

SURPRISE? I WAS dumb when Horace shoved the gun in my middle. And still I didn't tumble.

"Watch that, you fool! There against the wall! Take them!"

Horace kicked the guns on the floor out of the way. "Stand still!" he said, and the falsetto squeak in his voice was suddenly a man's baritone. "I'm tired of looking at you," Horace said nastily. "For two cents I'd bend this gun over your head and call it a night." He prodded me hard.

What was there to say? Horace had made a sucker out of me. He was the inside man for the Riorgen mob. No wonder they knew everything. And I, Mike Harris, the wise guy, had tipped my hand to him.

The three against the wall recovered their guns. Riorgen was highly amused. "Good work, Sammy," he said approvingly. "I was wondering when you'd get back. How's everything downstairs?"

"Quiet. What shall we do with this fellow?" Horace kneaded the gun muzzle against my middle again. "I got that big slob, Hauptman, again, by telling him to run out to the front gate to see if the police were coming."

"The boys at the gate will take care of him," Riorgen said. "Are you sure this Hauptman isn't wise?"

"I asked him what he knew," Horace said. "All he could babble was 'crooks.' He didn't seem to know any more."

I was getting sicker. Our ace card had turned blank. If Hauptman would be stopped at the front gate, then Kelly had been. Those hard-boiled guards belonged to Riorgen. The cops weren't coming after all.

Riorgen said softly: "Then this guy is the only one who knows who we are?"

"That's right," Horace nodded. "And he can get up in court and swear us all to the chair."

"*If* he gets to court," Riorgen said mildly. "And we don't want to take him away with us."

"The lagoon," Horace said under his breath. It had a world of meaning.

Funny, hearing your death sentence so casually. I had no illusions. Either I went on the spot quick or they burned later on.

Jake Riddle was the boy I swore at then. That ornate pass he had sent around to the hotel had been a pass to death. The best I could hope now was that Trixie wouldn't be dragged into it.

Horace thought of her at the same instant. "I haven't been able to locate that girl from the Blaine Agency," he admitted.

"We'll spot her now," Riorgen grunted. He turned to me. "How was the girl dressed?"

"Like an Indian squaw."

"There is no one downstairs dressed like that," Horace said flatly. The four of them were ringed around me now.

Riorgen struck a match, grabbed my left hand, held the flame under a nail. It was agony. I opened my mouth to gasp. A fist smashed it shut.

Riorgen dropped the match on the rug and stepped on it. "How about it?" he asked me pleasantly.

My own medicine was coming back. I didn't like it any more than the other fellow had. But he had hopes of living. I didn't. And I figured I could stick it out for Trixie's sake.

"I've been up against this before," I jerked out. "I know all the tricks. I'm not talking. Go ahead."

Riorgen said casually: "Plenty of time, boys. Take him out to the boathouse an' work on him. Nobody'll hear him squawk out there."

"I'll go," Horace offered quickly.

"I need you here. Out the back way, boys. And if he gets noisy, let him have it. And if you see Mae, tell her to come up here."

THE MOOR AND the Pirate grabbed my arms and led me out. The last thing I heard was Riorgen to Horace, curtly; "Bring up that dame with the diamond choker."

We went to the back stairs. As we passed the bedroom, I envied the fellow inside. He would see the sun rise.

Halfway down the stairs they released my arms.

The Pirate growled in my ear. "You're walkin' between us, see? We're all friends. Get it?"

I shrugged, nodded. If I could live a little longer by keeping my mouth shut I'd do it. No one we would meet could help me anyway.

And then as we neared the bottom of the stairs my heart turned over, my mouth went dry. A slender figure in the hall was staring at us through a veil. The snake ring on her finger was plainly visible. Trixie had waited for me.

I couldn't even look at her lest they become suspicious.

The Pirate spoke. "What're you hangin' around here for, Mae? Riorgen wants you."

She nodded silently. And as they took me on she was still there, slender, silent. And I knew Trixie knew I was on a spot, and was helpless. Kelly was gone. Hauptman was gone. I couldn't even warn her about Horace.

Outside I talked to them—anything to keep my mind off Trixie. "Seems to me you fellows are going to a lot of trouble tonight. Why didn't you line the guests up and frisk them in a hurry? You could have done it all in half an hour and been gone."

"An' that shows how dumb you are," the Pirate sneered. "It'd take a hundred men to cover that house an' watch the chauffeurs outside. Somebody'd give the alarm. Half the patrol cars in Chicago'd roll here. Say—we organize the house, pick what we want an' take it nice an' easy. We'll be gone a coupla hours before anyone tumbles."

"You can't take it all this way."

"We're pickin' what we want," he boasted. "The stuff we're leavin' ain't worth the trouble."

We were talking across soft turf under the wan moonlight. Once more the party was fading behind. I caught myself listening to the distant music. It would be the last music I'd hear, the last moon I'd see overhead, the last trees swaying in the breeze. For I knew too much and this was the end of Mike Harris.

We came to the lagoon, placid, waiting. The white swans were huddled against the opposite bank. The Moor spoke under his breath for the first time. "Smoots oughta be around here."

"Never mind Smoots. We don't need him. Over here."

They took me to the boathouse, shoved me in. And with the door closed, the light on, time turned back. In vivid memory I saw Walsh slumped in the boat seat—where I might be shortly.

"What happened to Walsh?" I said.

"In the lagoon with a chunk of iron under his belt," the Pirate grunted. "And now how about that dame? How's she dressed?" They grabbed my legs, chucked me to the floor. The Moor bent one of my fingers back, back....

Hurt? Sure—and it would hurt worse when he broke it. Through clenched teeth I said: "Go to hell! I'm not talking!"

That drew me a rap on the head with a gun barrel. Dizzy, bleeding, I still couldn't kick. I'd handed the same—and now I had to take it.

The Pirate growled: "Don't knock him goofy. He'll talk quicker if he feels everything."

And through a haze of pain I looked past their legs and saw the boathouse door opening slowly. Trixie's face peered in. And Trixie whisked inside with her toy automatic out.

11

RED-HEADED NIT-WIT

THEY FELT THE draft, heard her. The pressure went off my finger as they shifted around quickly. An oath from the Pirate.

"What are you doing out here, Mae?"

In a tense, husky whisper, Trixie answered. "Quick! In the house! Riorgen wants you both! Trouble! I'm to watch him!"

I forgot to breathe as I looked up at her. She couldn't get by with it. They'd spot her voice, her mannerisms, ask some questions that she'd stumble over.

I was all but forgotten now as they faced her. The Pirate rasped: "What's wrong?"

Trixie shook her little head behind her veil. "Riorgen says to run!" she whispered in such frantic urgency that I almost believed something was wrong. And they knew it.

"Okay," says the Pirate. "Maybe we better sap this guy first. He ain't told us how that female dick, from the Blaine Agency looks. We got to find her, an' it looks like we'll have to croak him before he puts the finger on her."

"Riorgen'll tell you about it," Trixie flashed. "He said for me to hold this man for you."

They left at a run, slamming the door behind them.

Trixie waited a moment and then looked out after them. "It worked," she said with a giggle.

I was on my feet then, caught her arm. "You little idiot, they might have got you too!"

"Mae is a blonde. I studied her voice while I locked her up and she swore at me," Trixie chuckled. She cocked her head on one side. Her dark eyes met mine over the veil. "So you wouldn't tell them what I looked like, Mike? How did they get you? What were they going to do?"

"Outside first," I said.

And not until we were well back from the boathouse did I speak. "Miley," I said rapidly, "is one of the gang. The guards at the gate are Riorgen's men. Kelly never got out. The police aren't coming. I knew too much and they were shutting my mouth."

"And first they wanted to know about me," Trixie reminded softly.

"Never mind about that. I wouldn't turn a dog in to these killers."

It was the wrong thing to have said. Trixie turned wildcat again. "Conceited as always, Mike Harris!" she flashed. "And now that I've gotten you loose, what does that massive brain of yours propose to do? It will probably be wrong! I'm going to the house."

"You're going to stay out of there!" I said, dragging her back. "I need you. We're trapped. The fence is high and burglar-proof. We can't pass it. The only way out is through the gates—and Riorgen's men are on watch there."

"So," said Trixie with acid sweetness, "you're going to grow wings and fly over, I suppose?"

"Maybe. Let me have that toy pistol."

"No," said Trixie.

I took it from her.

"Now," I said, "go slowly to the back gate and stall with the watchman. Give him the same sauce. Tell him Riorgen wants him."

"And suppose he won't listen?" she asked.

"Give it to him and leave the rest to me."

"Which probably means the finish for both of us," Trixie sniffed. But she went.

And I ran toward the house, cut across the path to the back gate and came in toward it from the other side, on my toes, noiselessly. Trixie was there talking with the watchman when I slipped up behind the little stone sentry box.

The watchman was growling: "It sounds funny to me. What does Riorgen want me to leave the gate for? Lemme see your face. You sound funny to me. Come on, pull that veil down."

He was standing over her, hand on her arm, shining a light in her face when I looked around the corner of the sentry box.

"No!" Trixie refused.

He pulled her veil down, and startled anger spouted. "You ain't Mae! *No you don't, girlie.* Stay here! We'll see about this!"

"Sure we will," I said, sliding up behind him with Trixie's little gun.

He wilted without a scrap. His gun felt good in my hand. "Here," I said to Trixie, returning hers. "Beat it out that gate and hunt a telephone at the nearest house."

"What are you going to do?" Trixie asked, hesitating.

"Trip Riorgen yet. He's probably wise now that something's wrong. It'd break my heart if Horace got away. I owe him a slap on the wrist for being so deceitful. Run!"

Trixie vanished through the gate, and I took the flashlight and found the real gateman a prisoner in the sentry box, tied, gagged and doubled up in the tiny area of floor space.

RIORGEN'S MAN CUT him loose. And while I talked fast to the ex-prisoner we locked Riorgen's man in the little stone edifice. Windowless, it was better than a cell.

My new man was stocky, powerful enough, but his round, flat face looked rather simple. And he was mad clear through. He broke into an explosive account of how they had surprised him.

"Can you lock this gate so no one can possibly get out?" I asked.

"Huh? Sure! Gotta chain an' pick-proof lock in there."

He unlocked the sentry box, stepped on Riorgen's man and came out with a length of case-hardened steel chain and a big lock. In a moment he had it in place on the gate. "The devil couldn't get out there now," he growled, turning to me.

"How many other gates are in this fence?"

"Just the main front gate."

"Come on then. I may be able to use you. Any other men around the grounds?"

"One man at the front gate."

"Was at the front gate," I corrected. "How brave are you, big boy?"

"I got two wounds in the Argonne," he said. "Both of them was in front."

"Fine. Maybe we can find another. Let's go."

We ran, skirting the north of the house. Riorgen must be tipped off by now, but I was banking on Riorgen figuring anyone loose on the grounds would be bottled up by his gatemen. He'd have to round up his gang first.

The house looked calm, peaceful enough in front. They were still frolicking inside. It was fantastic, in view of all that was happening. Something like a nightmare. But there was nothing dreamlike about Danny Riorgen.

The light was still on at the front gate. The two guards were lounging there with gun belts around their coats. I stopped among the trees and blackness north of the larger sentry lodge.

"Cut over to the driveway and walk to the gate like you're leaving. They'll stop you. Act dumb. They'll probably grab you. Let 'em."

"What are you going to do?" he came back at me.

"Never mind that. Keep them two guys talking."

He turned it over in his mind a minute, shrugged, said: "Okay." And then hurried over to the driveway.

And I slipped toward the sentry lodge. It had a window in the back, closed but not locked. Blackness, quiet were inside when I slid it up. Voices were speaking out by the gate as I crawled in. A match cupped in my hand showed three bound figures on the floor at my left. Two were in costume. I said: "Keep quiet. This is Mike Harris." And went to work on the nearest—Kelly.

Ungagged, he started to swear.

"Shut up!" I whispered. "You've clowned this act enough. Get over by the door an' get ready for trouble."

Near us a side window was open an inch or two. Outside

it a sedan was parked. A harsh, metallic voice suddenly began to issue from the sedan.

> *Calling all cars… Calling all cars… The Danny Riorgen mob is holding up the Free Milk Ball at the Leander Witherspoon house on the north lake shore. All cars rush there. Homicide has been committed. These men will kill… Shoot at any resistance. Allow no one to leave the grounds.…*

Trixie had got her call through!

The voice at the gate suddenly ceased. A man ran to the open car window where the radio was repeating the police warning.

He listened a moment, rasped: "It's a tipoff, Buck! The boys will be leaving in a minute! Throw that punk in there outa the way!"

Automobiles roared into action near the house. Riorgen's other cars carried police radios also.

I had just freed Hauptman when the door burst open. My stooge from the back gate was shoved in by one of the gorillas.

Thud.…

That was a gun hitting the back of the stooge's head. He dropped like a poled ox. And out of the blackness Kelly dived at the gorilla's legs and brought him down on top of the limp form. A gunshot crashed out. Kelly yelled. And Hauptman, big and burly, jumped into the mess.

A tangled pile of heaving, cursing bodies filled the doorway. I couldn't tell who was who, couldn't use a gun, do anything to help. So I waited, watching out the door.

The noise brought the second gorilla running. It took

him a second or two to understand what had happened. Then he jumped to the doorway with lifted gun, ready to shoot. I shot first—twice.

HE STAGGERED TO one side, out of sight. Perhaps to wait. Throwing up the side window, I dove out.

By the house the automobile motors were jazzing fast and loud. Headlights gleamed out, lurched ahead as two cars raced through the gears at top speed and rocketed down the driveway toward the gate.

I had intended to chain the front gate also. No time now. I didn't even know where the chain was. For a moment I was stumped. One gun couldn't stop those killers in their race for safety. And then, suddenly, I knew what to do. Trixie Meehan had done it once for me, in Palm Beach. I slipped into the sedan. The ignition key was in. A spin and the motor caught.

The radio was still broadcasting staccato orders that reached me in an unintelligible blur as I raced the motor. Down the long driveway two pairs of headlights were hurtling. They must have been doing forty or more already. Police sirens on them were wailing warning to the men at the gate and any traffic outside.

I let the clutch in. The sedan leaped forward, reeled around the corner of the lodge on two wheels as I yanked on the steering wheel. I caught a confused glimpse of the man I had shot lying beside the lodge door. Headlights were rushing at me, hopelessly close, as I wrenched the wheel again and placed the sedan broadside across the gate.

There was no time to open the door and jump. The first car crashed into me at full speed, siren screaming its futile warning.

The sedan turned over. Both cars brought up in a hope-less mess of wreckage that filled the open gateway. And the second car, reeling out of the drive, crashed through shrubbery and smashed into one of the massive gate pillars.

Bruised, dazed, cut with flying glass, I squirmed out from under the steering wheel. The sedan was on its side. Its interior was filling with the pungent fumes of spilled gasoline. Then—puff—and a sheet of flame shot up. In the other car a man screamed in agony.

The door above me, which had taken the full crash, was jammed shut. I kicked a hole through the top and forced myself out, still hanging on to my gun. I came up outside the gate. The leaping sheet of flame was rising higher, spreading swiftly through the wreckage. Men had tumbled out of the other two machines, were shouting, yelling hoarsely.

And as I staggered upright I heard from two directions the wail of police sirens closing in.

The footwalk gate was jammed shut. The only way out was past the blazing wreckage. A weaving, blood-smeared figure took it, clutching a sub-machine gun. The eerie red glow picked him out clearly. It was Danny Riorgen trying to break out with what was left of his gang. Danny Rior-gen—no longer cool and smiling in his gay costume. By the weird light of the mounting flames he recognized me, jerked up the submachine gun.

And I emptied my gun into Danny Riorgen just as the first police machine raced up and stopped with a squeal of brakes. Riorgen wilted, dropped, the gun falling from fingers. I ducked in the shelter of the sedan and waited.

Several shots greeted the police piling out—then

silence. Standing up, I saw figures running back through the grounds. They were trying to escape by the rear gate.

The coppers rushed up to me. Swiping blood from my face with a sleeve, I pointed. "There they are! Trapped in there! Now catch 'em! The back gate is locked! They can't get out that way!"

"Who the devil are you?" one of the coppers yelled.

"Just a private dick, from the Blaine Agency. You birds can have what's left of the party. I'm heading back to Times Square," I told them.

They looked at me as if they thought I was crazy. But just then the second police car sirened up.

They waved it around to the back of the grounds.

But I wasn't crazy. I said as much to Trixie half an hour later after a small army of police and dicks had combed the grounds and rounded up the last of Riorgen's gang and the million or so of jewels they carried.

"Back to New York for me," I swore to Trixie. "And the first bird who tries to stop me is going to run into mayhem, manslaughter and homicide. I'm going to get that vacation of mine and some peace. I'm fed up with trouble."

"You might," Trixie suggested, "stay over a day and take me to lunch tomorrow."

"Not if you were the last woman left."

"Oh, yes?" Trixie flashed bitterly. "But I'm not! There are plenty waiting to make you look foolish, Mike Harris! Furthermore, you might have been killed blocking that gate! Look at your face. Of all the red-headed nitwits, you take the...."

And so the battle was on again as we started back to town.

www.ingramcontent.com/pod-product-compliance
Lightning Source LLC
Chambersburg PA
CBHW031214020726
47499CB00002B/577